THE COMPLETE FIRST SEASON

J. H. GLAZE

ISBN: 978-0-9839069-7-1

Cover Concept, Artwork and Design: J.H. Glaze
Text Editing: Susan Grimm
Stock Image: Innovative Captures/Bigstock.com

First Printing March 2014
Published by MostCool Media Inc.
"Make it interesting. Make it MostCool."

Proudly printed in the United States of America.

First Edition March 2014

10 9 8 7 6 5 4 3 2 1

About RUNE: The Complete First Season

"This story grabs you by the throat and doesn't let go! From the first page to the last we are taken through a whirlwind of action and carnage as Jake discovers more about his transformation with the aid of his sidekick, a "dog" named Pete. "

— Author Lucian Barnes

"Yet another brilliant effort by an author who seems to be able to switch from one genre to the other without losing either his recognizable unique style nor his credibility."

- Author Christoph Fischer

"Glaze clearly knows the concept of a cliffhanger, as he stopped the episodes quite abruptly and right at a point which leaves you screaming, "No, I want to read more, now!"

- Library at the End of the Universe

"This book is set up as much for character development as world building. It is an amazing read, and I cannot see who would not like this book."

- Wanda's Amazing Amazon Reviews

"Takes you on a roller coaster of excitement, then leaves you at the peak, waiting for what happens next. Glaze is easily becoming the master of cliff hangers. I want to yell and cuss, but he knows what he's doing. He leaves you begging for more."

- Heather Badgwell

If you enjoy this story, you may want to try the full-length novels, novellas and short stories written by JH Glaze. Available on Amazon.com & other online retailers in eBook and Paperback.

Adult Horror:

The Paranormal Adventures of John Hazard Novels

The Spirit Box: John Hazard Book I

NorthWest: John Hazard Book II

Send No Angel: John Hazard Book III

Ghost Wars: John Hazard Book IV (*Coming 2014*)

Short Stories

The Horror Challenge Volumes I-III

Special Novellas:

Forced Intelligence: A Novella.

The Life We Dream: A Novella.

Serial Novel: YA & Adult

RUNE: The Thriller Series:

Visit the websites and pages of JH Glaze:

www.JHGlaze.com

https://www.facebook.com/JHGlaze.author

Follow on Twitter: @themostcoolone

Search for JH Glaze on Google for more!

Thanks For Reading! Reviews on Amazon and other sites are greatly appreciated.

"Destiny is like a creature of the night. It comes to you when you least expect it and is usually uninvited."

J.H. Glaze

RUNE

Episode I: Awakening

ONE

The balding man's eyes went wide with terror as the smooth leather soles of his dress shoes failed to grip the ledge of the brownstone building. He was stranded, standing four floors above the sidewalk and to the left of the open window. He pressed his back against the wall and dug his bloodied fingertips into the spaces between the bricks in a desperate attempt to keep from falling as he shuffled further away from the carnage that was unfolding inside the apartment.

The evening had not gone as expected. It was to have been a celebratory gathering of distant relatives and associates. Instead, there was nothing short of an orgy of gore and destruction going on inside the room he had only just managed to escape. Now, he was stranded on this ledge within earshot of the carnage. He could hear the screaming, howling, and wailing as each guest, someone he had known most of his life, was beaten, eaten, and torn to shreds just a few feet away.

Earlier, he had complained that the wool suit he had worn was much too heavy to wear indoors at such a crowded gathering, even though the air outside was rather cool. Now he stood there sweating with his eyes closed tightly, a single drop running down his forehead to find its way in between his clenched eyelids. He winced as the salty liquid stung his eyeball and, risking the loss of balance, he wiped his face nimbly with the sleeve of his jacket.

On the sidewalk below, a large black dog was barking incessantly. He wondered whether something down there had gotten it worked up, or if it had spotted him on the ledge. Either way, it was likely that the noise would attract the attention of the creatures inside the apartment unless he could get the beast to shut up.

He opened his eyes and reached into the pocket of his trousers in search of something to throw at the troublemaker. Maybe he could scare it off. Relieved to find some coins, he wrapped his fingers around them and pulled them out. Carefully, he tilted his head forward to locate his target. He could see the Labrador retriever with its yellow teeth barking up at him as it hopped from side to side.

Pausing for a moment, it walked in a full circle and then began barking again. If he had not been so distracted by the screams coming from the window next to him, the man might have noticed the unusual cadence of the barking. The woofs would speed up, and then slow, sometimes adding low growls. The subtle variations of pitch closely imitated that of human speech.

He felt sure that the damned dog was going to get him killed and prayed that he could make it run away. It was going to be tricky to cock his arm back and throw the coins with enough force to hit the dog without losing his balance. He decided to toss them underhand.

As the coins rained down, the dog yelped and jumped back. This had been his only chance, and he was grateful that he had hit his mark. The bastard stopped barking and stood with its head tilted as though considering its next move. It sniffed around at the fallen coins, and looked up at the man again. Baring its teeth, the hair on its back stood up as it let out a low growl that escalated into a frenzied barking fit once more.

"Shut the hell up!" he hissed, but the dog would not stop.

Cursing the beast for not giving up, he could see that it was even more agitated than before. It jumped up toward him managing to clear the ground by nearly three feet. For one startling moment, he locked eyes with the dog and thought he recognized something almost human, a distressed look of terror. Was the dog trying to warn him of something? Was it looking straight at him, or something above him? Either way, he'd had enough of it.

Slowly, he tipped his head to the side trying to see whatever was above him. Was it his imagination? Could he be dreaming up some dark creature in the shadows clinging to the bricks over his head? He shivered as he tried to get a better look. Without warning, two clawed hands shot out of the dark to lift him by his head from the stone ledge.

Screaming in agony at the viselike grip on his temples, his neck stretched and strained with the full weight of his body hanging below him. His mind reeled as the powerful creature dangled him over the ledge. Of course, he wanted to break free, but the knowledge that he would only plunge to his death kept him from giving into his natural impulse to thrash around.

There was a terrible cracking sound as the monster's long hooked talons penetrated his brain. The demon let loose an ear-piercing shriek as it crushed the man's skull with no more effort than it would take to squeeze a tomato. His head collapsed with a loud pop. Howling, the crazed monster tossed its victim away from the building allowing his body to drop to the sidewalk below, barely missing the dog.

Satisfied now, the beast surveyed the results of its work, watching as the dog darted into the shadows of a nearby alley. Letting out one last howl, the demon scrambled back through the open window to

join in the final throes of the chaotic carnage still
taking place inside the apartment.

TWO

Jacob Rowan was headed toward the door at the rear of the grocery store when he found himself accosted by the store manager.

"Jake, hey bud, I'm glad I caught you."

The tall man seemed somewhat intimidating with his dark piercing eyes and hulking frame, but Jake always tried to overlook his outward appearance and focus instead on the man's character. He had always treated Jake fairly, but the strange expression on his face tonight caused the younger man to take a second look.

"Yes sir, is something wrong?" Jake wiped his hands on the red apron he was wearing and untied the string at the front to remove it.

"No, son, not at all. I just wanted to give you this. I know you're taking tomorrow off, and to be honest, I... I mean *we* wanted to give you this before you left today." He seemed more awkward than usual as he shoved the white envelope into the boy's hands.

Jake looked around for the rest of the *"we"* his manager had mentioned, but no one else was there. "Uh... okay."

"I meant to say that, well, we all got together to get you something for your bir... well, just open it then."

Jake threw his apron over his shoulder and took the envelope from his boss. It was marked "For Jake" in neat block lettering. Flipping it over, he carefully opened the sealed flap and pulled out the card. On the front was a picture of a dog sitting by a fire hydrant. It read, "Somebody mentioned you turned 18 today."

As he opened it to read the inside, a gift card fell to his feet. He was happy to see that it was for the electronics store where he had been eyeing a new sound system over the past few months. Stamped on the display card attached to it were the words, "Fifty Dollars," in large letters.

"Wow, thanks!" Jake smiled as he picked up the card and peeled it from its backing. He looked at it again before shoving it into his pocket.

"Aren't you going to read the card, Jake?" His boss sighed with a bit of frustration that the card had been mostly overlooked.

"Oh, yeah... sorry."

He opened the card again and looked at the series of vignettes printed inside the card. There was one of a dog pissing on the fire hydrant, and another showed the dog biting a mailman. Yet, another scene was the dog taking a crap on the carpet in the house. Finally, the dog was pictured sniffing another dog's butt with a caption that read, "Don't do anything I wouldn't do!"

Every blank spot on the card had been signed. Most of the handwriting was illegible, but he could make out a few of the names. As far as he could tell, more than the handful of people he worked with regularly had signed it. He wasn't quite sure how he was expected to react but forced a laugh.

"Thanks, this is really cool!"

He wasn't lying. The gift card, indeed, was cool. The birthday card, on the other hand, well...

His boss grinned from ear to ear. "I picked it out myself. I thought it was hilarious. 'Don't do anything I wouldn't do,' and he is sniffing another dog's butt. Get it?"

"Yeah, it's really funny."

He could imagine the boss sniffing someone's butt, the guy in the produce department to be exact. Now he felt like laughing, and there was no use holding it back. He let it go. The boss laughed with him until he dissolved into a fit of coughing. Once his cough subsided, he finally gave Jake permission to go.

"Well, it's getting late and you probably want to get home. I'll finish locking up." He walked off in the direction of his office.

In the employee's break room, across from the loading dock, Jake paused for a moment at the small white picnic table and looked at his card again. He hadn't noticed before, but there was one important signature missing. He told himself that it didn't mean anything. Maybe his girlfriend, Maire, had not been at work when everybody else signed the card, or maybe someone had forgotten to ask her. Maybe he was making something out of nothing.

"Whatever," he said aloud, holding his apron in his hand as he went to his locker.

Mylar balloons floated out as the door opened. Jake grinned. Now he knew why she hadn't signed the card from the group. Taped to the back of the door, was a card and on the top shelf sat a single cupcake. He took out the small cake to have a look at it. It was colorfully decorated with the number eighteen hand-squeezed in icing.

"I guess that explains it."

Relieved, he smiled as he hung his apron on the hook. He pulled the card from the locker door and tore it open. It was quite different from the one his coworkers had signed. In fact, it must have been handmade since it had a photo of Maire on the front with the words, "I wanted to give you something special for your 18th", carefully printed in blue ink.

He stared at the photo. He had never seen her in a bathing suit before. She looked pretty hot for someone typically so quiet and demure. This was his girlfriend. He still couldn't believe it. Just last year he had been depressed about moving to a new school during his junior year and not knowing anyone... *again*. He and his grandmother had been moving every two years. Each time, she said it was because the economy was better in the new town. Since she did not have a job anyway, it didn't make much sense to him. Fortunately, he had developed a system for settling in quickly. His new school was no different. He had been quickly accepted.

Slowly, he opened the card to read what she had written on the inside. He was surprised to find lip prints. "A kiss to hold you over until I see you next. Your gift will be delivered in person at my house on Friday when my parents go out of town."

That made his heart jump. Was she thinking what he was thinking? If so, Friday was looking to be a very good day. He glanced at the calendar hanging on the wall, the one with all the recipes for dishes using a popular soup as one of the main ingredients. It was only Tuesday.

Jake laid the card on the shelf next to the cupcake and went to the sink to wash up before leaving for home. His hands still smelled like fish from cleaning out the display case where the fresh fish were kept during the day. He could see the clock as he applied the hand soap. It was 11:40. He was running late. His grandmother had asked him to be home before midnight. If it had not been for the last minute birthday celebration, he would have made it on time. He hoped she would understand.

After cleaning up, he went back to the locker, put on his jacket and left the birthday cards in the locker. He was careful to cover them with some papers, lest one of his co-workers find the one from Maire and use it to tease him. He would take them home later when he had his backpack with him. Snatching up the cupcake, he peeled off the wrapper and took a bite before heading to the front of the store.

His boss spotted him on the security monitor as he passed through the frozen foods aisle and got up from his desk. Jake heard the keys jingling and knew he was on his way to unlock the door for him. He took another bite of the cupcake and reached the door at exactly the same moment as the taller man. The key slid easily into the lock and there was a solid *thunk* as it released. He smiled as he pushed the door open.

"Hey Jake, it's pretty late. I'm almost done here. I can give you a ride if you want."

"Nah, that's okay. It's only a few blocks. I'll be fine."

"Are you sure? It's no trouble."

"Yeah, I'm good. I like the walk." With that, he slipped through the door and out into the shroud of night.

His boss watched until he was out of the parking lot before returning to his desk to shut down his computer. He reminded himself to lock the safe before he left for the night.

THREE

Jake walked home from work nearly every night. He was quite aware that the thirteen-block trek was nothing compared to the long commute that others had to travel to and from work. The only time he dreaded it was in the middle of winter or when it rained. Neither was the case tonight. However, there was something.

He couldn't put his finger on it, but there was an oppressive feeling in the air. The darkness was somehow darker, the shadows somehow deeper, as though something was lurking just outside of sight. He almost wished he had accepted the ride. Picking up his pace, he began whistling, a feeble attempt to overcome the tingly feeling of dread working its way up his spine. The tune echoed off the buildings as he walked along. *Hold that thought.*

Echoes? He stopped. It was never this quiet around here, ever. Even at three in the morning, there should be some ambient noise drifting up the block at least, an argument, a party, or the traffic from the main streets. There was always something going on in this neighborhood.

Jake looked around. "Something isn't right about this."

He tried to sharpen his senses. Perhaps he had just been distracted by the whole birthday present thing. He had to admit that finding the surprise from Maire had gotten him worked up. The promise of something special over the weekend, well, that had stirred both his imagination and his libido.

By the time he stepped onto the curb at the corner of the fifth block, he was relieved to hear a car coming up from behind. Even so, everything was suspect at this point, and as the Honda passed, he was surprised to see his boss waving at him from the driver's seat.

The car continued down the block, turning at the next street. Too late, Jake wondered if he should have flagged him down and taken advantage of that ride after all. He had not realized that his boss traveled down this street on his way home. He had assumed it would have been out of his way to give him a lift home.

In the distance, a church bell began to ring out the time. *It must be midnight*, he thought to himself as he picked up his pace. *I should have called and told Grandmother that I was running late. She's probably worrying herself crazy.* If he had a phone like most of his friends, he would call her right now.

As the bell struck ten, Jake began to feel an odd burning sensation in his feet. Two more rings and the burning so intensified that he was having trouble walking. A few steps from a covered bus bench, he tried leaning in that direction hoping that the momentum would work in his favor. Instead, he dropped to his knees.

He was feeling dizzy. The sensation was also affecting his hands as well as working its way up the back of his neck. It felt like someone had doused him with gasoline and set his back on fire.

"Help! I'm on fire!" he cried out in pain, hoping someone would hear and offer some assistance.

His vision blurred as he made his way toward the bus bench. From the shadows, something was approaching. Was it a dog or something else? He was seeing double now. Was it one or two of them? When he reached the bench, it was all he could do to crawl up and lay there on his stomach. He felt as though he was going to throw up and most of his body was wracked with burning pain.

The dog approached cautiously, sniffing the air as it came closer. Slowly it circled the bench, stopping near Jake's head. It stood looking at him, tilting its head from side to side. Jake did not move as the dog started to bark. It was not the full loud bark of a dog about to attack. It was more like an attempt to communicate with him, maybe to get him to sit up.

"What are you looking at, dog? Go get me some help!"

Jake yelled at the creature as though he expected some TV act of canine heroism, but the dog only stood there growling.

"Go, will ya?"

The dog quieted for a moment, staring at him in silence before beginning again. "Wrrrrofff, Wrr… nothing anyone can do to help you, I'm afraid."

"Aaaawwwwwwwrrrrr! Did you just speak… like in words?" Jake spoke to the dog through clenched teeth.

"What do mean… *just?* I've been speaking ever since I walked over here. It's not my fault you couldn't understand me until now."

Jake's hands clenched into fists as he desperately tried to ease the unbearable burning sensation. "I need help, dog. Unless I'm hallucinating, I'm begging you to go and get someone. Hurry, I think I'm dying here!"

"You're not dying, you're changing. Oh, and I'm very real." The dog sat back on its haunches and casually scratched behind its ear with an experienced hind leg.

"Changing? Into what?" He spoke louder than he intended as he tried to deal with the pain.

"Look at your hands. You should be able to see it by now."

As a matter of fact, he did see something. It looked like smoke, or maybe it was steam, seeping between the fingers of his clenched fist.

"Oh shit." He opened his hand and turned it over. "Oh shit, oh shit! What the hell?"

"What do you see?" The dog moved closer and tried to get a look at his palm.

"Get away!" He swung at the dog. "Did you cause this?"

The dog sat down and made a face resembling a frown.

"Actually, no, this was bound to happen whether I was here or not. I just thought I'd come by and help you get through it."

"Help? How are you going to help? Are you a doctor?" Jake let out a groan and arched his back.

"I could lick it if you want."

"Arrrgghh, no, how would *that* help?"

"I've heard that a dog's saliva has healing properties."

As if to emphasize the point, the dog raised its paw and began licking it.

"Of course, that could be a myth. You still didn't tell me what was on your hand, by the way."

"Well, the burning is starting to ease up some."

Jake opened his hand to look at it again. "Owwww, there's some kind of mark."

He opened his other hand. "There's one on this hand too."

"So, I don't get to see them?"

The dog casually looked away as though it didn't matter, but quickly turned its eyes toward Jake again.

"What do they look like, exactly?"

"Here, you tell me, smart ass!"

Exasperated, Jake held his hands out so the dog could see his palms.

"Ahhhh, I see. You really are him then."

"Him, who? What?"

"You are the… this is gonna sound cliché, I'm afraid, but I've waited a long time to say it."

"Well, say it then, dammit!"

"You're the chosen one." The dog appeared to be grinning.

"Chosen for what?"

The pain was fading, and Jake sat up on the bench to look the dog square in the eyes.

"Well, they've used so many names when discussing you, arbiter, authority, exterminator… the one they've been waiting for… and here you are!"

"Who are *they*? What are you talking about, dog?" He stopped.

Now that the pain and burning had lessened considerably, he was coming to terms with the fact that he was actually talking to a dog.

"I'm losing my mind. I can't be having a real conversation with a dog."

"Sure you can. Especially, since I'm not *really* a dog." The dog stood up and turned in a circle. "I'm just trapped in this one."

"Look, this is crazy. I'm talking to a dog that is trapped in a dog, and I'm the Terminator. I need to go home!"

"Ah, home. Did you live in an apartment on the fourth floor? Brick building? About eight blocks from here?"

"Hey, how do you know where I live?"

The dog lowered its head. "I had a feeling you lived there. That was why I went there earlier tonight. I sensed that you were going to need help, but you weren't there. Good thing."

Jake leaned forward on the bench to get a better look at the dog. It seemed twitchy or blurry somehow as though its face was changing or... morphing? It was moving, fading in and out.

He rubbed his eyes to clear his vision, but when he looked again, it was the same. If he looked away, everything around him appeared to be normal, but every time he looked at the dog, he could see the same blurring and twitching.

"What's wrong with your eyes, boy?" The dog cocked its head.

"I'm seeing something on y... no, maybe *in* you. It keeps moving or changing."

He reached out and touched the dog's face, but he couldn't feel any movement or anything unusual at all. The dog sat back on its haunches and lifted its front legs up, resting its paws on his knees.

"You can see me in here?" It waved its head from side to side. "You see something besides the dog, don't you?"

"I don't know... Yes... I do... I think. What is it? It looks like a girl's face, sort of. Are you a ghost?"

"Not a girl or a ghost." The dog sounded disgusted. He put its paws back down on the concrete and turned its back on him. "At least you can see the real me."

"If you're not a dog or a ghost, what exactly is the *real* you?"

"Okay," the dog said as it turned back around. "I'm going to tell you this, but don't freak out on me. I'm a demon."

The dog barked the words in a hushed muffled tone, almost a mumble, more like a woof.

"A what?" Jake scrambled to lift his legs off the ground and quickly slid backward down the bench.

"Yes, you heard me. You can put your legs down now. I don't bite."

The dog bared its teeth in another yellowed smile.

FOUR

A lone police cruiser pulled up to the brownstone apartment building. The two officers had received a domestic disturbance call ten minutes earlier. "Hey, what's that on the sidewalk? Looks like somebody's having a bad night."

The driver shifted into park and unfastened his seatbelt. "Call for an ambulance... and backup," he shouted as he jumped from the car. His partner was already on the radio as he walked up to the crumpled body. "Sheeeeeit!" The man's head was misshapen, crushed on the sidewalk by the fall. "Looks like we got a jumper."

***

Jake had lapsed into silence as he walked toward home. As long as the dog wasn't threatening, there was no reason to chase it away. After the strange occurrences of the night, he felt better with the animal by his side. Besides, the dog seemed to know something about what and why this was happening to him.

Only a few blocks from his apartment, the creature still followed quietly behind him. Quite certain now that Jake was headed to the same place where the man had been thrown from the ledge less than a half hour before, the dog was about to drop the bomb.

"Hey, uh, Jake." It trotted up next to him. "Look, I don't think you should be going home right now."

"Oh yeah? Why's that?" The boy was getting frustrated with all the mysterious undertones and stopped to confront the dog as he spoke.

"What's your name anyway? Or should I just call you Dog."

"Dog would be fine, but my traditional name is Gerlock."

"Gerlock, huh. That's traditional?"

"Indeed. If you must know, it is a very old name."

"Okay, well, we can discuss that later. Right now, I need to get home." He headed down the street again. "How long do you plan on tracking me, Gerlock?"

"I am here to assist you to the end."

The dog walked up next to him, trying to slow the pace. "I've got to say it once again, do not go home right now."

"Look, Gerlock, my grandmother's probably worried sick. I should have been home hours ago."

Gerlock stopped in his tracks. He was determined to keep Jake from going any further. Anyone witnessing the scene would have simply seen a dog sitting on the sidewalk barking very loudly at the man in front of him, but now Jake could understand every word.

"You can't go home. It's not safe for you there. Listen to me!"

That got his attention. He turned around and went back to the dog.

"Exactly what do you mean by 'not safe'? You need to tell me what you're talking about, right now. No more games."

"Everyone in the fourth floor apartment that you call home… everyone who was there is gone."

"Gone? As in *went somewhere else?*"

The dog looked down at the sidewalk before letting it fly.

"They're all dead, Jake."

"They? Who are you talking about? Who is dead?"

The terrible news was slowly beginning to sink in, and his head began to spin. Stepping back against the nearby building, he propped himself up to keep from falling.

"What are you saying?"

"The time of your transformation had been long awaited, Jake. Your handlers travelled here from faraway places to witness your passage into the Awareness. They were waiting for you to return home when the huskers arrived."

Jake fell weakly to his knees and yelled at the dog. "You're wrong. My grandmother is not dead! She can't be. What do you mean by *the awareness,* and what are *huskers*?"

"I know it is a lot to take in all at once, but you must hear the truth. There is no time to waste now. The old woman, though she cared for you for many years… she was not your grandmother. In fact, she was not related to you at all."

In the young man's eyes, the dog recognized the first signs of trouble. He was about to run, but the dog continued.

"The *Awareness* is the change you've been going through since I found you. There are demons that reside inside people in this world and can control them completely. They have no physical body of their own. They're all around you, Jake. You just weren't able to see or sense them before."

"Huskers, on the other hand, are much more powerful and can appear human in order to mingle unnoticed. They don't require a human host. They create a shell resembling a man or woman. They wear it like a husk, but when they're about to attack, they shed that exterior like a snake. It was huskers that killed your people."

Jake cautiously rose to his feet, his gaze locked on the dog. "This is crazy. Either I'm dreaming, or I'm having some kind of allergic reaction to something."

"Or you're on drugs," Gerlock volunteered.

"I don't do drugs." He glared at the dog. "I'm out of here. I'm going home."

"Wait. Before you go, there's something else."

The dog closed in trying to block his path of escape.

"When you were a child, wasn't there a lot of travel and discussion about history, ancient ruins, religion and philosophy? Didn't you receive training in some kind of martial arts? Didn't the woman who said she was your grandmother tell you what happened to your parents?"

Jake couldn't take any more. He bolted past the dog in a full sprint for home. As he rounded the corner at the end of his block, he saw the flashing lights of police cars and an ambulance. He avoided the yellow plastic tape strung across the sidewalk and went straight for the door.

Tears streaming down his face, he punched in the security code and flung open the door. As he flew up the stairs, the cops on site did not attempt to stop him. They shook their heads as the large black dog following behind him plunged through the spring-loaded door. Gerlock was lucky it did not crush his tail as it closed behind him.

Though winded after four flights of stairs, Jake discovered he had adrenalin to spare. He ran down the hall to his door and was relieved to find that it was locked. If anything terrible had happened in there, surely the door would have been left unlocked.

He dug in his pocket for the key, hoping to find his grandmother alive and well.

As he pulled out the key, blood began to seep from under the door. He realized his optimism may have been for nothing. The dog arrived in time see him insert the key in the lock.

"Don't open it, Jake!"

Jake was confused. Standing there shaking, he wondered if he was ready to face what was behind that door. Did he really want to know where the blood was coming from?

"Hey, what's that dog doing in here?" Down the hall, a neighbor had opened his door and stood there in his boxers and a wife beater shirt.

"It's nothing. Go back inside your apartment. You didn't hear or see anything," Gerlock ordered.

All the man could hear was the dog growling, but he obeyed the command.

Visibly disturbed and pale, Jake wasn't sure what to do.

"My grandmother could be hurt. Someone might be needing help in there."

"Remember what I said, Jake. She was not your grandmother. She told you what you needed to hear about who she was, about who you are. Keep that in mind if you insist on opening the door. There is no hope in that apartment. You can't help them now."

"Maybe I should go back down and get the police. I could have them to go in first."

"Did you get a good look at them before you came up here?" The dog sniffed at the pool of blood expanding from beneath the door. "If one of those cops is a husker, he might finish what they came to do. They came here to kill *you*, Jake."

"Why would they want to kill me? If I can't even trust the police, what am I supposed to do?"

"If you're going to be around the police, you need to be in a place where they can't get you alone."

"The police station, there'd be cops everywhere."

"Lock the door, Jake. Let's go."

"I can't. I can't just leave. What if she's still alive in there? What if you're wrong?"

"You should know the answer to that question by now."

"How would I know?"

"You've been transformed, Jake. There are things about you... well, you're different now."

The dog trotted down the hall.

"Follow me."

"But... wait up."

Jake followed him to the door of the man who was complaining earlier.

"What are we doing here?" he whispered.

"Take a deep breath, Jake, and allow your mind to clear."

"Now close your eyes and focus on the space inside." The dog stood behind him wagging its tail for encouragement.

"Now gradually move your head from side to side as if you're standing in the room and looking around."

"Oh shit. I can *feel* the guy moving around." Jake turned his head slowly. "He's coming closer... uh, now farther away."

"What you feel is his life force. Disconnect from him now and come back to your door."

The dog trotted back expecting him to follow. Standing before the blood on the floor, he looked back to see Jake standing at the neighbor's door with his eyes closed.

"Hey, come on. We need to get going."

"I can't move!"

He was frozen and unable to turn his head to see the dog approaching. As the dog reached him, it reared up on its hind legs and shoved him with its front paws. It was enough to knock him off balance and break the grip of the psychic bond.

"Wow, *that* was weird. How did you know I could do that? Better yet, how did you know how to get it to stop?"

"Sometimes you humans need a little push in the right direction. Look, Jake, you're not the only one of your kind I have worked with. There have been several since I made the choice to run with the good guys."

"Good guys? Who are the bad guys?" He followed the dog back to his apartment door.

"I'll tell you in a minute. Right now, I need you to scan your apartment."

"Can't you do it?" Jake was pleading.

"No. You have to sense this for yourself, so you can believe. Do it! We are running out of time."

Jake closed his eyes and focused his thoughts while the dog watched. His jugular began to protrude so much that it looked as if it would burst.

"I sense there are people inside, but it's not like the other guy. They feel... I don't know how to describe it. Cold, maybe? Nothing seems to be moving around."

"You are sensing the remnants of energy from those who had come here tonight. Do you believe me now?"

"Remnants? You mean they're all dead? Wait!" Suddenly, he grabbed for the door handle. "There's somebody alive in there!"

The key was in the lock before the dog could do anything to stop it. Click, twist, and the door was thrown open.

FIVE

Detective Mallory received the call twenty minutes earlier and had nearly reached the scene of the jumper. He was about to bust a couple of drug dealers when the call came, and it really pissed him off. There was no choice but to respond since his operation was 'off the books'.

He had planned to rob the scumbags and expected a decent haul of cash and meth from them. The interruption was a massive inconvenience, but he swore he would get the job done next time. As he pulled up to the scene in front of the apartment building, he could sense that there was more going on here than what he had been told by the dispatcher.

"What do we have here? Looks like somebody forgot their parachute," he mused as he climbed out of his car.

Flashing his badge for the street cops, he lifted the crime scene tape and stepped under it to get a closer look at the body of the victim. He circled around the sprawled corpse of the nearly headless man, and he occasionally bent down for a closer look.

"Any witnesses?"

He studied the faces of the cops and EMT's who were waiting for him to finish his assessment. A chorus of shrugs and headshakes was the only response he received from them. He grabbed one of the EMTs by the arm and pulled her closer to the victim.

"So, missy… I need your professional opinion."

Fishing an antenna-like pointing device from his pocket, he pulled out the end and extended it to a full three feet.

"You're not supposed to... uh..." she started.

Using the tip of the pointer, he probed what remained of the man's head and moved some bits of brain and skull to one side. The damage was so severe that his face looked more like a rubber mask that had been laid on top of the gore.

"I'm thinking this guy might have been dead before he hit the pavement. The way his body is positioned, he couldn't have landed headfirst. It looks like his head was crushed before he fell. Or, maybe he was thrown from the building. What say you, sweetie?"

He looked directly at the woman, but she was looking away from the body.

"Excuse me, I asked you a question."

He took hold of her chin, applying pressure until she was forced to turn her head and look at the crushed mess of the victim's head. Mallory could see the look on her face, half shock, half anger.

"I'm sorry, honey. Is this your first jumper?"

He grinned wide and looked to the crowd expecting laughter, but his joke had fallen flat. He nudged her back toward her partner.

"Go on, you can have him in a few minutes as soon as I get some... what's that?" He raised his head and sniffed at the night air like an animal. "Sumbitch!"

Abandoning the crime scene, he bolted up the steps prepared to enter the apartment building only to encounter the locked security door. The rest of the public safety team stood scratching their heads and looking around. He hadn't said a word before he disappeared.

SIX

Jake's mind was reeling as he stood outside his grandmother's apartment looking in. It was hard to tell how many people were dead in there because pieces of bodies were scattered everywhere. The blood seeping under the door appeared to come from one of the largest pools closest to the door. There was blood all around, and the walls were splattered and dripping with gore.

"Don't go in there. You must not leave any evidence that you were here. Don't touch anything."

The dog tried to block him with its head, but Jake was not attempting to advance. He stood riveted to the floor.

"What h-h-happened here..." He was barely able to say the words.

"They killed everyone to prevent them from helping you," the dog quietly responded. "You were meant to be here for the ritual. If you had been here as you had promised, your remains would be splattered on the wall along with the rest, and the world would be headed for destruction."

The dog's eyes shifted and its ears perked up. "To your right, Jake, look!"

"Jacob, get away from here, my boy." It was his grandmother's voice.

She strained to pull herself across the slick floor. There were gaping wounds where her face and body had been slashed. She was pale, her graying hair matted with blood. Bent at awkward angles, one of her arms was obviously broken. Sharp bones poked through her translucent skin. He wondered how she could move at all. Suddenly, she pushed with her legs and slid to the door so rapidly that he nearly jumped back. Instead, he stooped down to reach for her.

"Grandmother... I don't understand. What's going on? I need to call... an ambulance." He spoke haltingly, trying to overcome the grip of grief that was forcing his throat to close.

"It is too late for me, Jake. I'm already dead," she gasped. "I have willed my soul to remain in this body until you arrived." With great effort, she reached into her sweater and took out a key hanging from a fine gold chain around her neck.

"Everything you need to know, for now, is hidden away in a safe deposit box in your name at the First National Bank. The rest you must seek for yourself. This is your fate, your purpose... and, Jacob, the account is in *your* name... Rune. Your given name is Jacob Rune." With great effort, she pulled on the fragile chain to break it and handed him the key.

Jake took it from her hand as her eyes went dim. She lay in the pool of blood that had oozed ahead of her as she crawled across the floor. He bent to touch her forehead. Just then, a crash of breaking glass from downstairs caused him to jump.

"I know you're confused, Jake, but we have to go. Right now!"

The dog latched onto his shirttail, nearly pulling him off balance. Letting go of the shirt, it barked, "Is there some other way out?"

"Huh? Yeah, follow me." Tears streamed down his face and he strained to keep from sobbing. He couldn't afford to lose focus on the problem at hand.

He straightened and shoved the key into his pocket as they rushed down the hall to the door marked Exit. Franticly, he pulled on the door handle only to find that it was locked.

"Damn!"

The dog was pacing in circles. "Got any other ideas?"

"The apartments on that side of the building have fire escapes, but we can't get to them without going through one of these." He pointed toward the door where his agitated neighbor lived.

"You mean the asshole who yelled at us? Knock on his door."

"He isn't going to invite us in and let us climb out through his window."

"Stop arguing and get him to the door!"

They hurried back to the neighbor's door and Jake banged with his fist until it opened.

"What the hell is your problem, man?"

***

Detective Mallory was short of breath by the time he reached the landing of the third floor. His knuckles were bleeding from punching out the glass on the door below and were dripping onto the tiled floor. He leaned against the wall and gathered his strength while pulling a shard of glass from his hand.

Any *normal* detective would have asked the others downstairs to watch his back, or keep an eye on the exits while he went after his suspect. Unfortunately, he wasn't exactly *normal*. The two demons in possession of his body had forced him to go after the boy alone.

"I gotta lay off the donuts," he said to himself as he bounded up the last flight of stairs. Reaching the top, he drew his weapon.

***

"Step aside, and allow us to enter," Gerlock commanded.

Immediately, the man did as he was told. Jake hadn't noticed before but, whenever the dog barked an order at this guy, his voice seemed to swirl and softly repeat in echoes. It must be some type of mind control, but it didn't matter. The only thing that mattered was that they get to the fire escape as quickly as possible.

Jake locked the door quietly behind them. It freaked him out not knowing exactly how close their assailant had come. Had he reached the top of the stairs? There was no way to tell without keeping the door ajar, which was definitely not an option. In the meantime, the dog continued to instruct his mental slave.

"Sit over there and be quiet." The dog nodded toward the sofa. Again, the man obeyed.

Jake went to the window. It was tight, but he managed to pull it open. Turning to the dog, he tipped his head motioning in the direction of the window. "Let's go."

Then it hit him. There was no way for a dog to climb down a metal ladder. "How are you going to get down the fire escape? Are you going to stay here and try to control that cop?"

"Well, Jacob, if I was able to do that, would we be hiding in this apartment? No, I would have made that ass-hat buy us some breakfast." The dog's bark dripped with as much sarcasm as a dog could produce.

"I need to get out of here as much as you do. Good as I might be at mind control, I can't manipulate someone who is possessed. I think this guy is carrying more than one of my cousins inside of him." He looked out of the open window. "And probably more than one gun."

"So, what do we do?"

Jake didn't want to abandon the dog. Certainly, he had been useful so far, and he knew at least some of the answers to the questions Jake had about his predicament.

"You'll have to carry me," the dog casually replied.

"Down the fire escape? On the ladder?"

He felt sure that would be next to impossible. The dog had to weigh at least seventy pounds, but it seemed the only way.

"This body wasn't exactly built for grasping a ladder, if you see my point. So, are we going to stand here and talk, or are you going to throw me over your shoulder and get on with it?"

***

There were six doors lining the hallway, and the detective started at the end nearest the top of the stairs. He put his ear to the first door listening for any movement. There was no sign of occupants. As he raised his foot to kick in the door, he caught a whiff of something he had detected from the sidewalk, the smell of blood and something stronger. It was definitely the scent of an enemy.

"Damn."

He stopped himself just before his foot hit the door. Instead, he walked further down the hall with his weapon drawn and ready. He froze when he saw the blood on the floor in front of Jake's apartment.

This time he didn't hesitate. He kicked the door in and lost his footing on the blood-slicked carpet in the process. Falling face first through the doorway, he landed unceremoniously on top of Jake's grandmother's body.

"Shit!" he exclaimed, rolling off the dead woman and into the sloppy gore that was congealing on the floor.

No matter where he placed his hands to push himself up, he could not avoid the blood. As he looked around the room, his eyes took in the tremendous amount of shredded flesh, brains and guts splattered over everything. Under normal circumstances, he would have been mortified at what he saw, but in his current state, motivated by the influence of the demons within him, he found himself intrigued by the work of his peers.

"Reminds me of Picasso. What a true genius," the evil living inside of him muttered aloud as he rose to his feet.

***

Jake and the dog looked down from the fire escape. If either had a plan, they would already be on the move. Jake glanced at his companion. He had no idea how he was going to get them both down safely.

"Look, we need to get out of here. Give me some idea how I can carry you. I can't just throw you over my shoulder."

"Right, let me think."

They looked again at the metal stairs.

"I think I can navigate the steps if you steady me. Hold on to my collar."

"I was wondering why a demon dog would need a collar.

"Because we're in the city. Please, can you focus on the problem at hand?" The dog was getting anxious and the chitchat was not helping to calm him.

"Alright, alright, let's just do it."

Taking Gerlock by the collar, they began their descent. At first, the going was slow. The metal steps were narrow and each paw had to land just right so as not to slip. As they continued, they became more surefooted and were able to pick up their pace. Once the final landing was reached, the real problem became evident.

***

Mallory stood outside the neighboring apartment, which moments earlier had been the route of Jake's escape. After what he had just been through, he dreaded kicking in another door. Unfortunately, the demons within him were not about to wait patiently for someone to answer.

He backed up and ran at the door like a fullback running a play. The hinges broke away from the wooden trim, and the door fell before him as he exploded into the room. The man inside was quietly sitting on his sofa apparently still dazed and confused. Mallory was about to slap the guy into reality when he caught the scent of his prey wafting through the open window.

***

Jake kicked the latch that held the ladder in place, and it rattled as it dropped. There was a loud *thunk* when it stopped short, about a foot above the sidewalk. *How was he going to get the dog down the ladder?* Jake had an idea.

"Come here, dog." He unzipped his jacket to within two inches of the bottom as he squatted.

"There is no way in hell I'm going to fit in that jacket," the dog chided.

"No, really?" Jake responded sarcastically before patting his right shoulder. "Get up here and put your front legs over me here."

The dog let out a sigh and did as he was told. Jake put his hands under the dog's hindquarters and pushed him up.

"Now put your back legs into my jacket," he grunted.

"Are you sure about this? I don't put much faith in the strength of zippers," the dog sniped, but did as he was asked. Jake's jacket acted as a sling to support the dog, but his body was now in Jake's face.

"The hardest part is going to be getting onto the ladder. Try to hold on to my neck with your front legs."

The dog did his best to dig in his claws as Jake moved into position at the ladder. Grabbing hold of each side, he put a foot on the first rung, and then leaned back to shift the weight of the dog to his chest.

"If you drop me, I swear I'll bite you before I die," the dog grumbled as Jake inched his way down step by step. At the bottom of the ladder, he quickly lowered the dog to the sidewalk.

"Let's get out of here."

"We have to get rid of the cop first. He's got your scent. He can follow us now no matter where we go." The dog obviously had something in mind. He bolted down the alley toward a dumpster. "Follow me."

Jake was uncertain, hesitating until he heard the detective clamoring down the metal stairs above. He had no choice but to follow. Ducking behind the dumpster where the dog was hiding, he asked between breaths, "Now what?"

"Get ready, he's going to have his gun drawn. You'll have to knock it out of his hands, extract the demons and send them straight to hell. Then we'll be finished with this."

Jake was astonished. "Are you kidding me? How am I supposed to do that?"

"No time to explain, just get the gun out of his hand and do what I say."

SEVEN

Mallory leapt from the ladder and onto the ground, his nose turned up to sniff the air. He smiled. "I got you now, bitch!" Pulling his sidearm, he headed into the alley.

Steadying the gun with both hands, he checked side to side as he methodically worked his way to the dumpster. He was kicking piles of trash and checking doorways as he went. He knew he was getting close, he could smell them. Thinking that they must be hiding inside the dumpster, he inched forward, finger on the trigger. The smell of his quarry was very strong. Gripping his gun in one sweaty hand, he reached for the lid of the dumpster with the other, flipping it open with force.

As quietly as he could, the dog woofed, "Now!"

Jake came roaring from behind the dumpster and body slammed the detective. The impact dislodged his gun and sent it sliding along the concrete. "Now what?" Jake yelled at the dog as he struggled on the ground with the large man.

"Slap him twice on the forehead with the palm of your right hand. Hurry, before he regains his balance!"

Jake didn't argue. He opened his right hand and slapped the detective on the forehead with his palm.

"Raaaawrrr!"

The force of the evil scream blew Jake's hair back. He watched in terror as a gnarled face split away from Mallory's head.

"Hit him again!" the dog yapped.

Jake immediately responded with another slap to the forehead. Another face, even more disgusting than the first, appeared on the opposite side of the cop's head. The demons jerked and twisted as they strained to re-enter their host.

Jake had the cop in a tight grip, his left hand clutching his bloody shirt. He struggled with the weight of the man as he held him up to keep him from falling. Mallory's face was slackjawed and empty.

"Let go of the body and grab those bastards!" The dog nervously paced back and forth, as he franticly barked orders at Jake. "Push them down to the ground after he falls and hold them there with your left foot."

Even though he didn't understand what he was doing, Jake complied with everything the dog told him. Letting the man's body fall, he grabbed hold of the two heads. Although they appeared translucent, Jake was surprised to find that they were very solid indeed. The demons snapped at him with horrid sharp teeth as he stepped away ripping them both straight out of Mallory's body as it slumped to the ground.

The fiendish spirits in his hands writhed like snakes as he forced them to the ground and stomped on them with his left foot. Screeching, they tried every way to break free but were unable to get out from under it.

"They aren't as big as I expected when they're out of the body. What do we do now?" Jake looked down at what appeared to be two of the most ugly five-year-old children he had ever seen. They thrashed about wildly, stretching to bite his leg with their snapping jaws.

"If there were only one, we could interrogate, but you won't be able to hold them down for long. We need to send them back where they came from." The dog stood behind him now as though seeking protection.

"You think you can stop us, Gerlock?" one demon hissed. "You have no idea the havoc you have brought upon yourself."

"The human will be skinned, just as his ancestors before him. You will live to enjoy the show, dog dweller, and then we'll deal with *you*. After we tear you to ribbons, we will serve you up to the master like a bowl of linguini," the other spewed from its foul mouth.

Jake was terrified. He had no idea how he could be holding onto such vile monsters, and he was sure he didn't have a clue what to do next. He was relieved when the dog finally stood on its hind legs with its front paws on his back and began talking him through it.

"Repeat after me, Jake," the dog growled. "Loremi ipsom dolor sitat amet."

Jake hesitated as he tried to make sense of the words.

"Say it, Jake."

The dog waited for the boy to repeat the words. He watched as the spirits under Jake's foot began to shake and wail as though experiencing the most excruciating pain.

"Ut enim ad minum lo veniam," he continued, and Jake repeated.

As the last word was uttered, Jake was blown off his feet. He landed hard on the ground a few feet away as the screaming, twisting demons rose into the air in a small vortex of trash and dead leaves. Within the miniature twister, the evil entities exploded into flaming particles that burned away like bits of tissue paper. Then, all was quiet in the alley as the debris settled to the ground.

EIGHT

Trembling and exhausted, Jake pushed himself up from the pavement. He stood there in a state of shock as the dog sat nearby licking its paw.

"Nothing to it, Jake. Just another day at the office."

"What? Are you freakin' kidding me? What just happened here? And now, what do we do with *him*?" He motioned to the cop in his bloodstained clothes, who lay moaning and shuddering on the ground.

"We help him up. He has no idea what happened or how he ended up here. We'll just brush him off and send him on his way."

"He's covered in blood and you don't think he'll notice something is wrong, or remember that he was trying to kill us?"

"Did you ever see that movie about the alien hunter guys all dressed in black? They had something that looked like a pen and they flashed it to wipe people's memories?"

"You mean the one about the secret government agency? Now that was a movie!"

"Yes, it's just like that. This guy has no idea how he got here. Those ugly bastards had him totally under their control. To them, he was just a body to use at their convenience. Look on the bright side, Jakey boy. You really did him a favor. Probably even saved his life by ridding him of his demons."

The dog stood up and made his way toward the detective. "Now let's do him another favor. Even though he won't remember what happened here, he'll remember seeing us. We want to be remembered as the good guys." He nodded toward Mallory who was rubbing his head with a bloody hand. "Think fast, Jake. I have a feeling you'll know exactly what to say."

Dubious, Jake walked toward the man. He offered him a hand, and the cop gladly took it as Jake helped him to stand.

"What's going on here? Where am I? And who are you?"

"My name is Jake, sir. My dog and I were passing by this alley when we heard some noise, like yelling. We came over to see what was going on and found you here lying on the ground. Are you injured? You have blood on your clothes."

"I don't get it. I don't feel wounded and I don't remember coming here. Did you see anyone else around when you found me?"

"No sir. Are you sure you're all right? Is there someone we should call? Do you need help getting a taxi?"

"No, I can get someone to come and pick me up. Thanks for helping me. Most people don't want to get involved." He looked at his hands and muttered, "What's with all of this blood?"

"Glad to be of help, sir. Oh, uh, is that your gun?" He pointed at the weapon.

"Oh man, yeah. Thanks again for helping."

Mallory went to pick up his gun while the boy and the dog walked off toward the street.

"No problem, glad we could help." Jake called over his shoulder.

NINE

After a long period of silence, the dog finally brought up the obvious. "Shouldn't we find some place to spend the rest of the night? It's probably not a good idea to be wandering the streets. It's one thing for a dog to be roaming around at this hour, but you should not be out so late. The streets get more dangerous the closer it gets to sunrise."

"I know. I'm thinking. I'm sure I don't have enough money to get a motel room, and even if I did, there aren't any around here."

"Do you have any friends nearby that we could stay with until morning? Or maybe you, like me, have betrayed your own kind and now you have no friends?"

"Well, dog, I'm definitely not like you. But as far as friends go, I don't have one that would appreciate me knocking on their door at this time of night." He thought again. "Except… Maire. We could try going to her house, it's just a few blocks from here. One time she suggested that I sneak out at night and go over to her place. I didn't think it was such a good idea at the time."

"I think we should head over there as soon as possible before we get ourselves into any more trouble. You lead, I'll follow."

The dog was ready to get far away from this area. He was sure that more trouble would be headed their way if they lingered. At the next corner, Jake took a turn into a more sparsely populated area. There were fewer apartments and more family dwellings.

"Hey, dog, I know we talked about your name before, and you said your name was Gerlock, but I think we need something more normal sounding if we are going to be going places together."

"Yes? What were you thinking?"

"How about Spike?"

"Seriously, Spike? Is that all you got? How about Freud?"

"Like the psycho psychiatrist? That doesn't make much sense."

"It makes more sense than Spike!"

The dog stopped to urinate on a fire hydrant while Jake walked ahead.

"How about a simple human name?" he called after him. "I've seen dogs with human names, like Jake, for example." The dog grinned and ran to catch up with him.

"If we're going to use a human name it should be a one syllable name. I hate the singsong of calling a dog with more than one syllable in the name. Do you know how ridiculous a guy sounds saying, 'Here Sebas-tian,' or some crap like that?"

"Look, you call me that and I *will* rip your leg off. That's a promise," the dog snarled.

Jake stopped and looked at his troublesome companion. "I've got it. How about Pete? It's short, masculine, and it rolls off the lips."

"Pete, huh? I guess I could live with that, but no nicknames. Not Petey, Pete-ster, or anything like that. Just Pete, alright?"

"We're here." announced Jake, ignoring the dog's comment. "Be quiet while I get her attention... Pete."

TEN

Pete followed him to a back window on the ground floor behind the house. From the outside, all they could see through the glass were the colorful striped curtains that hung closed on the inside. Jake stepped up through the surrounding bushes and gently tapped on the window. There was no sign of any movement. Another tap and the room lit up from behind the curtains. A hand cautiously drew them back.

Maire peeped through the gap and saw Jake standing in the bushes. Immediately, she yanked the curtains all the way back. She looked tired and a bit perplexed standing there in her pajamas. She motioned with her finger and mouthed, *One minute*, then turned and walked away to shut her bedroom door. When she returned to the window, she reached up to unlock it. After a brief struggle, she slid the lower section up.

"What time is it? Are you crazy?" She reached for her phone to check the time. As the display came on, she said, "It's 2:30 in the morning, Jake! What's going on?"

"Let us in, we can explain everything." He motioned toward the dog.

"Us, we? You mean the dog too?"

"It's okay. He's house trained. It's not like he's going to mess up the carpet."

He turned to Pete and asked, "You won't, will you?"

The dog replied with feigned innocence and flashed one of his toothy grins.

Maire stuck out her head and looked around. She turned and listened for any sign of her parents. "Come on then, but be quiet."

As Jake lifted the dog up to the window, Maire crossed the room again and locked the door. The dog was already inside as she turned around, and Jake was climbing through right behind him.

"Be careful not to make any noise. My mom will probably kill me if she catches you here." she whispered. "What's going on, Jake? Why are you out in the middle of the night, and I didn't even know you had a dog."

"He's not really *my* dog. Look, I don't exactly know how to explain everything. If I tell you, you're gonna think I'm crazy."

Pete came up behind him and nudged his leg. "Go ahead and tell her the truth. I *really* have to see this."

All Maire could hear was Pete growling. She took a step back.

"Well, Jake Rowan, it sure would be nice if my boyfriend actually shared what's going on with his life, especially when he and the dog I didn't even know he had are standing in my bedroom at this hour. Why is he growling? He doesn't bite, does he?"

Silence. Jake was trying to figure out how to tell her the story. He wasn't sure how much of the truth she could handle. In the end, he decided to start with the small stuff. "Well... this is Pete. I, uh... kind of got him for my birthday."

"Oh, I'm sorry. Happy birthday!" She kissed him on the cheek. "Continue, Mr. Shroud of Mystery. You got a full-grown, old dog for your birthday? Who insulted you with that gift?"

Pete growled softly and sniped, "You're not so special either, sweetheart." He tilted his head, his eyes growing wide. "Jake, we have a problem. There's at least one or two of them nearby."

Jake bent closer to the dog. "What? Are you sure?"

"Are you talking to that dog? I mean... like actually having a conversation with it?" Maire stood with her hands on her hips. "I'm seriously worried about you, Jake."

"I guess I'd better tell you everything I know so far. You'll either believe me or ask me to leave."

He straightened up to find her eying him, waiting.

"I'll start with this," he offered, showing her the palms of his hands.

"Since when did you get tattoos?" She took his right hand in hers and looked at it up close.

"They're not tattoos really." He shuffled his feet and cleared his throat. "Okay, so around midnight, I started having pains all over my body and then these marks just appeared."

"So what are they? And, all over your body, where else?"

"My hands, my feet, my neck and back. It felt like fire when it was happening, but thankfully it only lasted a few minutes."

"This is some serious crap. Turn around, I want to look at your back." She looked concerned.

He hadn't even thought about what could be on his back. He took off his jacket. When she pulled his shirt up to his shoulders, she covered her mouth with her hands and sat down on the bed. "Jake, your back is covered with those things!"

"What? Let me see." He went to the mirror on her dresser and looked over his shoulder. "Oh shit, what *is* that?"

Pete walked around behind him to get a better look. "Tell her those are runes," he growled. "It appears that you have some information there. I can't read or I'd tell you what it says. It's some ancient text, though. Too bad I never learned to read runes. They don't send us to school or...."

Jake pulled his shirt down and looked at the dog, "Ancient text? What kind of ancient text would be on my back?" His voice cracked with a tinge of panic.

"Jake, you are talking to a dog." Maire was growing pale. From what she could see, there was something entirely wrong with this situation, and it was only getting worse.

***

In the second floor bedroom immediately above them, Maire's ten-year-old sister Lisa, opened her eyes and sniffed at the air.

"He's in the house," she declared in a voice that bore no resemblance to her own. In fact, it wasn't human at all.

Lisa jumped from the bed leaving the blankets to flutter to the floor behind her. In seconds, she was out the door, down the steps and into the kitchen. She cocked her head as she looked around for something to use as a weapon. The demon inside of her knew that together they would not be strong enough to kill the enemy hiding in her sister's room. They would need something... sharp!

There was a blur as she flew to the sink. Shoving her hand into cold dishwater, she fished out a meat cleaver dripping and glistening with soapy water. *This should be enough to get started,* the demon thought as the girl walked toward her sister's bedroom. She was using the blade to chop at the air as though warming up for what she was about to do.

***

"You can only hear that he is growling and barking, right?" Jake tried putting his arm around her to calm her. She was beginning to shake, but she wanted no part of his reassurance and pushed his arm away.

"No, Jake, it's not that easy. You really think that dog is talking, don't you? Are you feeling ill? You sound totally crazy."

"Seems to me your girl is the one with issues, buddy." Pete grinned innocently.

"What did he just say?" Maire's voice was becoming shrill. "I want to know what he said."

"I thought she didn't believe I can talk," Pete sighed.

Jack frowned at the dog, and tried to smooth things out. "No you don't. He's being a smartass now."

"Yes I do! What did he say? Tell me or leave right now, Jake."

Suddenly, her tirade was interrupted by a frenzied knocking on the door. Maire looked at Jake in a panic, motioning him to get in the closet. Frantically, she pointed at the dog. "Take him too." She whispered so quietly, it was more like mouthing the words.

"Hold on a minute!" She called out and walked to the door.

"Maire, let me in." It was her sister calling from the other side of the door.

Lisa held the meat cleaver behind her back and waited impatiently for the opportunity to kill whoever or whatever was in that room with her sister.

Maire hesitated to unlock the door until Jake and the dog had hidden in the closet. She was relieved to know that it was her sister instead of her dad. Calmly, she called through the door, "Go back to bed, Lisa. It's late."

"But I'm scared. I heard something strange. Just let me come in and sleep with you for a while," she pleaded pathetically.

"Not now, Lisa. Everything's fine, just go back to bed."

At once her sister's voice distorted as the demon inside her demanded, "You let me in, or I'm gonna tell Daddy that someone is in there with you!"

Lisa's threat and the change in her voice left Maire feeling like she was riding a rollercoaster of panic and flying downhill. Should she open the door as her sister demanded, or should she let her rat her out to their dad and get it all out in the open?

"A tattooed boyfriend, his so-called talking dog and almost three in the morning," she muttered to herself as she made her decision and turned the small lock in the center of the doorknob.

***

From inside the closet, Jake could barely see through the slats of the dual doors. He sighed knowing that he was going to have to face the little sister who was always busting his chops. *"When ya getting married, huh? What's that lump in your pants, Jake? I'm gonna tell mom you guys were foolin' around."* She was such a pain.

Lisa stood in the open doorway, her tangled blond hair framing her dark-rimmed eyes and falling over her shoulders. She sniffed the air and bolted to the closet, raising the meat cleaver above her head. She slammed head-on into one of the doors. Swinging the blade with force, she hacked the slats into splintered bits, barely missing Jake's heaving chest. Stunned, Maire could only watch as her crazed sister brought the cleaver up again in an attempt to strike her now exposed boyfriend in the face.

Just then, a dark blur shot out of the shadows from the other side of the closet and slammed the little girl to the floor. The soapy handle of the blade shot from her fingers as her head thumped down on the carpet. Lisa was cursing and writhing under the weight of the dog, struggling to get hold of something to pull herself back to her feet.

"Hit her, Jake," Pete howled. "Forehead!"

Maire's legs felt like Jell-o as she tried to come to her sister's aid. Her mind was trying to process what she had just witnessed, and was finally catching up to the moment. Her sister had just tried to kill her boyfriend, and his dog had attacked her and now was about to kill *her*. She tried to speak but the only words she could force out were, "No, stop!"

Little Lisa lay squirming on the floor pleading for help as Jake knelt beside her. She was moving around so much that he couldn't be sure he would hit her forehead. He grabbed hold of her knotted hair in his left hand and slapped her straight on the forehead with his right. As the demon within her split away from her head, she let out a horrible roaring scream.

"Lisa... what the hell?" Maire was shocked and confused. "What is this Jake? Get him off of her." She realized she had better stop yelling and get hold of herself. With all of the noise, surely her parents would wake up and walk in on this chaos. Acting on autopilot, she slammed the bedroom door shut and locked it again.

***

On the second floor, in the master bedroom, Maire's mother sat bolt upright. She could hear the noises from her daughter's room filtering up through the ventilation system. Her husband continued to snore as she climbed out of bed and ran for the door. She went down the stairs and headed straight to Maire's bedroom.

***

Jake was pulling the demon from Lisa's body and holding it down with his foot as he prepared to recite the words that would send it to hell. Pete worried that he might not remember what to say, so he began, "Loremi ipsom dolor sitat amet," but Jake was already a step ahead of him.

Maire's mother reached the closed and locked door as he was finishing the last phrase. Rather than trying the doorknob, she ran straight through door, which exploded into the room in a shower of fragments and splinters. Looking down at Lisa, she yelled,"What's your problem? Can't you do anything right you stupid little girl?" She kicked her daughter's limp body, just missing the dog with her foot.

Maire stepped forward and touched her mother's arm. "Mom, don't, she's…" She was cut short as her mother's backhand caught her square in the chest, knocking her across the room. She bounced off the dresser and landed on the floor gasping for breath.

Jake was caught completely off guard and looked to Pete for a suggestion on how to handle this new assault. The dog didn't hesitate to provide one.

"Take that witch out! I'll hold this one until you're done with her." He took hold of the demon that Jake had nearly dispatched while he wearily rose to face the new and deadlier threat.

There was a fire burning in the woman's eyes. In a blur of blinding speed, she lunged for the meat cleaver lying on the floor and came up swinging. For a split second, Jake flashed back to several years earlier. He recalled dodging a blade very similar to the one that the girl's mother was now brandishing, her swing missing his head by mere inches.

***

Jakes grandmother had insisted, despite all of his objections, that he enroll in a martial arts class. "Nothing fancy," she had said. "Just something you might use to defend yourself when you're out in the harshness of the world."

After two years and countless tournaments, Jake had emerged from the class with four trophies and a black belt. He never thought he would actually need that training, but now here he was fighting for his life.

***

With two body blows and a roundhouse kick, he sent Maire's demon-possessed mother crashing to the floor. As she got to her feet again, it was obvious that her shoulder had been dislocated and her arm dangled at her side. Jake took a guarded stance as she burst out sobbing.

"I'm so sorry... I don't know what got into me. Please help me, I think I've broken something."

From where Maire sat leaning back against the dresser, she pleaded with him, "Please, she's hurt Jake, don't hit her again."

Her mother's good arm was down, but she kept her weapon hidden from view just behind her hip. Jake felt bad that he had injured his girlfriend's mother. He heard Maire pleading for him to stop and felt a twinge of remorse. When he stepped forward to help the woman, she immediately took her shot. The blade cut through his shirt leaving a two-inch gash in his chest. He could feel the blood running down his stomach as he jumped back into a defensive stance.

Now he was pissed. He wasn't about to give her another opportunity. As she stepped forward to swing again, Jake took hold of her arm and pushed it away, slapping her directly on the forehead.

The evil presence within her howled as the woman's head flipped backward and the demon's face popped straight out to take its place. Before withdrawing his hand, he closed it around the vile spirit and pulled it directly out of her body. The knife dropped from her hand as she crumpled to the floor where she stood.

Now Jake had a problem. Pete was a few feet away wrestling Lisa's demon, and the one he was clutching in his right hand was not about to go down easily. It was the strongest of any spirit he had yet encountered and snapped at him with a mouth full of sharp teeth.

"Bring that one over here," he yelled at the dog.

Pete was clamped down tight on demon's shoulder. He had braced himself in order to keep hold of the thing. Now he was concerned that it would get the better of him if he tried to move. He shook his head. Rather than taking the creature to the boy, Jake would have to bring the other one to him.

Jake could see the problem and tightened his grip. He jumped toward the dog, slamming down next to him, and threw the demon in his grip on top of the other one, knocking it from Pete's jaws. Reacting quickly, he stomped down on both with his left foot.

Now that they were under his control, Pete could breathe. "Say the words, Jake," he gasped. "I've had quite enough of these two. Could you please dispose of them so we can get some rest?"

"Uh, help me here, I can't remember all the words. Could you run me through it again for good luck?" He was as eager to get it over with as the dog.

ELEVEN

In moments, the two demons were dispatched and Jake was helping Maire sort things out. She was dazed and sobbing. It was obvious that she was shaken by what had just happened. She didn't even make a move to check her mother and sister's condition. Instead, she cried out, "Mom, Lisa, they're dead, aren't they."

"They'll be okay, don't worry." He tried to assure her as he helped her get to the bed and sit down.

Pete was sniffing at her mother, examining her for any sign of life. "She's alive. Looks okay, except for that shoulder. That's gonna hurt."

"See, Pete says your mom's going to be okay." Jake couldn't bear to see her in such a state of distress.

The dog went to Lisa as Maire leaned into Jake. Her sister was not moving aside from her shallow breathing.

"I'm going to have to wake this one." Pete started licking her face.

"Jake, you're cut." Maire noticed the rip in his shirt as she looked at him. Blood was beginning to seep through the thin fabric. "How bad is it?"

"I don't think it's too bad. It doesn't hurt at all now."

"Really? Let me see." She pushed his arm away and pulled up his shirt. Stunned, she moved closer to get a better look at his chest. She could see the remains of the bloody mess, but the gash from the knife was gone.

"What is it?"

"There's no cut here, just some blood. I don't understand."

Jake looked down at his chest. "Damn, that's cool!" He touched the spot where the gash had been. "You know anything about this, Pete?" he asked.

Pete was still circling Lisa, waiting for her to regain consciousness. "Well, I've heard of the healing before, but nobody I've worked with could do it... until you, that is. You are full of surprises."

He sat down and scratched his ear. "Don't go all cowboy on me, though. Scratches, cuts, maybe even a gunshot might heal, but you get something chopped off and it's not growing back. You're not a lizard."

"You really are talking to that dog. Can you actually tell what he's saying? All I hear is barking, growling and whimpering." She went on, "This is just so crazy. What about Lisa and my mom? Are you sure they're okay? What were those things you pulled out of them?"

"Demons. Ever since midnight, after I changed, I have some abilities that I didn't have before. And now, for some reason, people who are possessed by those things keep trying to kill me. That thing I did to your mom and Lisa is the only way to stop them, but I don't understand everything yet. I'm going to have to go to the bank in the morning to find out more about it."

"Demons? The bank? I don't get it."

"Grandmother gave me a key to a safe deposit box. She said everything I needed to know is in there."

"Hey, yeah, shouldn't you be at home by now? She must be worried sick."

He began to choke up as he told her, "My grandmother's dead, Maire. The whole apartment is full of dead people. I can't go there."

"Oh god, I'm so sorry." She put her arm around his waist. Then, as the rest of what he had said began to sink in, she leaned away from him. "Wait a minute… your apartment is full of dead people? What are you talking about? What happened?"

"Hey, Jake. I hate to interrupt, but we have a problem here. When this woman wakes up, she's going to be hurting and she will definitely be wondering what happened. I suggest we put her somewhere else before then." Pete was sitting next to Maire's mother.

"Shit, I didn't think of that. When they wake up they won't even know what happened." Jake stood up from the bed. "What are we gonna do?"

"I have an idea," Maire volunteered. "If you're sure they are okay, we can put Lisa in my bed, she'll wake up and she won't even know anything happened, right? But what about my mom? How will I explain her injuries?"

"Well, she did smash through the door. I think that's a real good explanation," Pete said with a smile. "Pretty tough woman to do that, but she did have help."

"Not good enough. Grab her feet, Maire." Jake bent over the woman and slid his hands under her armpits. "On three, lift"

"Where are we taking her?"

"To the bottom of the stairs. Maybe she'll think she was sleepwalking and fell." He began the count, "One… two… three…"

As he lifted, her shoulder made a loud popping sound and slipped back into place. They carried her to the bottom of the stairs and laid her there on her side with her feet resting on the bottom step.

They went back to the bedroom and put Lisa in Maire's bed. "When she wakes up, I'll tell her she came downstairs and asked to sleep with me. Now you and that dog have to go. I can't explain your being here."

"How are you gonna explain the door to your mom?" Jake nodded toward the pieces of wood scattered around the room. "And the closet?"

"She's been watching a lot of those paranormal horror movies lately." She feigned a look of total innocence as she rehearsed her excuse. "It just happened, Mom. It scared the crap out of me."

She looked at Jake, "Don't I look freaked out?"

Jake smiled, "Yeah I guess you do. Should I be worried that faking comes so easily to you?" Then he realized they had better hurry before the two of them woke up. "If we leave here at this hour, where are we gonna go?"

"I don't know, it's nearly four o'clock. Maybe the all night coffee shop? It's only two blocks away."

"Right, okay. Can I call you later?"

"I guess. I don't know, we'll see. Give me some time to process all of this crazy stuff." Maire looked at the mess on her floor and shook her head.

Jake was hoping for some sign that everything would be the same between them as it was before, but he knew it wouldn't. He could tell by the way that she was looking at him.

"Come on, Pete. Let's go get some coffee."

TWELVE

Jake sat inside the coffee shop, watching through the window while Pete patiently waited outside. He had wanted to bring the dog in, but one of the waitresses stopped them before he could close the door behind him. She did say he could wait just outside the door. He probably should have been relieved that she allowed him to sit that close to the door, but the dog had saved his life more than once tonight and he was feeling guilty about leaving him anywhere outdoors.

"Miss." He motioned with his hand as he called her. "Can I get this coffee to go, please?"

"Are you that worried about your dog? I see you watching him."

"Yeah, kinda. It's late for him to be out there, and we lost his leash and tags earlier today. I'm afraid if a cop comes by and sees that he doesn't have them, he'll call animal control."

"Well, I shouldn't do this, because I don't want to get in trouble. Is the dog trained? Would he stay under the table if I let him in?" She was standing there with her arms crossed. She sized him up, looking for any sign that he was lying to her when he responded.

"I'm pretty sure he'll do whatever it takes to get in here, if that's possible."

"Okay, you can bring him in as long as you are out of here before six. That's when the day manager comes in. Got it?"

Jake was already up and heading to the door. "I really appreciate this."

"Yeah, well, you better keep him quiet or you'll both have to go."

Jake got up and walked out the door. "Hey, Pete, she said you can come in if you stay under the table."

"Are you going to get me something to eat? I haven't eaten in more than a day. This dog needs food."

"Sure, what do you want?"

"Steak and eggs sounds pretty good." He licked his chops, thinking about it.

"I don't think I have enough cash for all that." He reached for his wallet and counted the few bills. "I can probably do a cheeseburger, and that'll about wipe me out. Can you make do with that?"

"A dog's gotta do, what a dog's gotta do." He got to his feet and headed toward the door of the restaurant.

"Hang on a sec," he said as he lifted his leg and relieved himself on one of the lights along the sidewalk. "Okay, let's do it. Food!" Wagging his tale, he followed Jake inside and to the table.

The waiting seemed like forever. As Pete ate his cheeseburger, Jake went over everything that had happened in these few short hours. While he had lived every harrowing minute of it, he felt as though he had been dreaming. More than anything, he wanted to wake himself up. If he were asleep, then all of this had been nothing more than a nightmare. Unfortunately, he was forced to accept that it had been quite real.

Well, at least he knew where he stood.

At about ten minutes before six, Jake paid the bill, leaving a small tip, and the duo headed outside. The sun was about half an hour from making its appearance. As they turned to walk down the sidewalk, Pete moved out about ten feet in front of Jake

"Hey, walk back here next to me. You're supposed to have a leash in town, remember? If you walk beside me, maybe no one will notice that you don't."

"I have come to the conclusion that you humans have way too many rules," Pete grumbled as he dropped back even with his partner. "I guess next you'll tell me that whenever I take a dump, you have to put it in a plastic bag and throw it in the trash."

"Damn! Is that what I have to do?" Jake wondered just how much trouble this relationship was going to be.

"Look, I'm not telling you to do it, but believe it or not I can hear some of this dog's thoughts. Apparently, that's what his previous master did."

"You can hear its thoughts? What else is it thinking?"

"Listen, this relationship is not about me being a middleman between you and the animal I happen to inhabit. Right now it needs to take a crap."

"I don't have a plastic bag. Go over there behind that bush."

"You're asking me to break the rules?" Pete looked at him in surprise.

"You're kidding me, right?" Jake stopped and crossed his arms.

"Sure, give a dog a minute," he grumbled and walked behind the bush.

Jake looked around to get his bearings while he waited. They were nearly sixteen blocks from the First National Bank, where they needed to go to get to the safe deposit box. He knew of a city park halfway to the bank. He planned to wait there until the bank opened, but he couldn't stop thinking about what might be in that box when they got there. It could be anything, or maybe not much at all.

Obviously it was something worth dying for. Grandmother had sacrificed herself for it, but what could it be?

"That felt good." Pete was wagging his tail as he came from behind the bush. "You know the problem with a spiritual existence?"

"Maybe you could enlighten me." Jake turned and started walking away as the dog trotted to catch up with him.

"It's the simple pleasures. Things like that cheeseburger earlier and a good crap. You just don't have those quality of life experiences in the spirit realm." His tail was wagging merrily as he rambled on about things that Jake didn't really care to discuss at that moment. "Where are we headed, anyway?"

"There's a park a few blocks from here. We can hang out there until 8:30 or so. Then we'll walk to the bank. That should put us there right about the time they open."

"Do you think they'll let me in? I've never been in one of those buildings."

"I'm guessing there are rules about that, too. If we're going to work together, we'll have to figure out a way to get around your handicap. Who knows what I'm going to find in that box. I just hope, whatever it is, it comes with instructions."

THIRTEEN

The duo sat in the park until 8:30 as planned and then headed for the bank. Jake was glad they had not encountered anyone while they waited. He also had come to realize how grateful he was for Pete. The dog didn't seem to get tired. He was constantly on guard for any possible danger. It had given him the opportunity to steal a much needed moment of shuteye.

They arrived at the bank just as the security guard was unlocking the doors. "Uh, good morning. I was wondering if my dog here could come inside with me while I check out my safe deposit box."

The guard eyed the large black dog. "Is it a service dog? It doesn't have any tag."

"Service dog?" The term wasn't entirely new to Jake, but he stalled and hoped that the guard would give in.

"I'm guessin' he ain't one. A service dog has a special harness and tag, and yours don't have neither."

"Is it okay if he sits outside over there then?"

"Long as he stays away from the ATM. I don't need people complainin' about a dog barkin' and growlin' at them."

"Thanks." He led Pete back down the steps to a spot on the sidewalk next to a bush. It was near enough to the bank but hidden from view unless someone was looking for it.

"Look, I can't take you in, but that doesn't mean I don't want to. Will you wait here for me? I don't know how long this is going to take."

"Sure, Jake. I've got nowhere else to go. Besides as long as you live, it's my sole purpose to protect you."

"I like the way you say that. *As long as I live.* Gives me a lot of confidence there, buddy." His words dripped with sarcasm. "So, with that in mind, if anyone comes by and they smell like they want to kill me, start barking as loudly as you can."

"You really want me to bark, Jake?" The dog stared at him blankly and offered a casual "Woof".

"That doesn't even sound like a real bark." Jake smiled as he walked back to the door.

"To everybody but you, it does."

As Jake entered the bank lobby, he was amazed by the marble floors and the columns. It was a beautiful old building and very nicely appointed. He stood for a minute looking around until one of the women rose from her desk and asked, "Can I help you, sir?"

"I guess so." He pulled the key from his pocket. "My grandmother gave me this key and told me that it opens my safe deposit box. I'd like to take a look in it."

"Certainly. Sit right over here and we'll find the box we need to get for you." She showed him to the chair in front of her desk as she sat down in her own. He waited while she logged into her computer. "Okay, what is your name, sir?"

"Well, I'm not sure which one she used. Try Jacob Rowan."

The woman typed the name and looked at her screen. "I'm afraid I don't have that name in my records. Was there another name?"

"Uh, try Rune."

"Just Rune?" she looked perplexed.

"Jacob Rune. She may have used that."

"Yes, here you are. Box 357. Please sign here." She wrote something down and then handed him the clipboard and a pen. She had neatly printed 'Rune 357' on the paper.

Jake signed next to his name and handed it back to her. "Can I keep the pen?"

"Of course you can. Follow me please, Mr. Rune." She stood from her desk and walked toward the large round vault door. Just past the heavy door was another one, and beyond it, some metal deposit boxes lined the walls. There was a table in the center of the room. The woman used Jake's key and her own to open the door to the box. Sliding the large container out, she carried it to the table.

"If you need anything, please let me know," she offered, excusing herself from the vault.

Jake stood and looked at the large box sitting on the table. Whatever was in it was the reason his grandmother had been killed and the extent of everything he had left in this world. He lifted the lid and opened the box with a feeling of sick anticipation.

"Oh… My… God!" He couldn't help but say it out loud. There were no other words to express what he felt as he looked into the box.

RUNE

Episode II: Nemesis

ONE

Jake Rune stood in the vault of The First National Bank. His hands shook as he prepared to open the safe deposit box that his grandmother had established in his name. It was her last words to him before she died. "Everything you need to know right now is in a safe deposit box at the First National Bank."

The carnage in the apartment where he had lived with her and the pool of blood where she had lain as she handed him the key to this box was a scene that would be etched in his mind forever. He was having a difficult time coming to terms with all that had happened in the hours since he had left the store where he worked.

Outside the bank, a large black Labrador retriever named Pete was patiently waiting. The young man was not his master nor his friend, but his chosen responsibility. Possessed by an ancient demon named Gerlock, Pete was fully aware that the young man he accompanied was more than human. He had the marks. He also had the gift. Most of all, he had a mission, and that was why they were here on this foggy morning. Jake needed to fully realize the significance of his mission.

Gerlock promised Jake that he would be there to protect him as long as he was alive. He regretted the way he had phrased that vow now as he remembered that the others who had come before Jake did not always live long after the Awareness. All versions of the legend held that one day the last of the demon killers would live a long and productive life. He would send the creatures of chaos back to their hellish world, the same terrible existence that they had waited so long to escape.

Jake was the one. If Gerlock had not been exiled by his own kind, he would have felt compelled to put an end to the boy's life himself. For him, living one day inside the earthly hosts was better than living an eternity in the world of suffering he had left behind. Even though the creatures he possessed eventually wore out or met their demise over time, he actually relished the experience of their death before he passed into the next one. The end of life experience held deep meaning to earthly beings. However, as horrible as the circumstances could be, nothing on earth was as terrible as the agony of everyday existence in his home world, a place of eternal torturous agony until the gateway to this world had been opened and he came here.

***

Inside the bank, Jake took a deep breath as he stood before the safe deposit box. It would contain everything he had left in the world except for the clothes on his back. According to his grandmother, he was about to find the answers to his true identity. Finally, he opened the lid.

His legs nearly gave out as the contents of the box were revealed. Immediately, his eyes fell upon the layer of neatly wrapped stacks of one hundred dollar bills. "Oh... My... God..." He gasped, trying not to allow his surprise to attract attention. His hands shook as he removed each banded stack and placed them on the table next to the box. In total, there were twenty stacks of fifty bills, five thousand dollars per stack.

As he piled up the cash, the remaining contents were at last revealed. Sitting atop the assortment of items was an envelope with his name neatly written in his grandmother's delicate hand. Carefully, he slid his finger under the flap to open it and drew out the letter.

Dearest Jacob,

If you are reading this letter, then it is certain that something has happened to prevent me from sharing this moment with you. I have taken the precaution of preparing for this day, and I'm quite certain that I will rest in peace knowing that you have found your way here. This box contains everything you will need as you set out to fulfill your life's purpose.

Many years ago, you were entrusted into my care in order that I might raise you in the disciplines you would require as you met your destiny. It has been a blessing and an honor to watch you grow these many years. I hope you can understand that even though I am not your grandmother, I have loved you as my grandson just the same. I have always wished the best for you.

Now as to your heritage, and this may be difficult for you to grasp...

"That's putting it mildly, Grandmother. I'd really be freaked out right now, or dead perhaps, if not for Pete and what little I have already learned." Jake shook his head and read on.

...You were born into a secret bloodline of advanced beings whose purpose is to rid the world of the demons that have preyed upon humans for thousands of years. You are not merely a hunter. You, my boy, are an exterminator. You will not simply track and kill these evil creatures. Your charge is to send them all back to the hell where they belong.

You will find the details of your mission within the pages of the ancient book inside this box. Written by your ancestors over the millennia, it contains knowledge that only you and your kin can understand. No permanent translation of this mysterious book exists, because its text evolves and is rewritten as the condition of the world changes and affects your challenge.

As difficult as it is to fully explain everything about the writings to you in this letter, it would have been impossible to do so before you came into the Awareness on your birthday. The truth is, even now, I am unable to read or understand what is written there.

In the envelope along with this letter, you will find a business card. Ben Cramer, a professor from Columbia University, is an expert in ancient languages and cultures. He has promised to assist you with the translation of the texts, including the markings on your body.

There is a scroll among the contents of the box. It belonged to your great grandfather. Guard it with your life, Jake. The demons will amass great power against you in order to possess it, but you must never let them take it from you.

I have included everything you need in order to travel to all corners of the globe if you should find it necessary. The future of mankind rests on your young shoulders, Jacob. I wish you the best. It was an honor and a pleasure to serve you. I hope I have adequately prepared you for your coming hardships.

Love, Grandmother

Tears flowed down his cheeks as he folded the letter and returned it to the envelope. He laid it on the table next to the box and closed his eyes, picturing her face. She *had* been his grandmother, the only family he had known. Except for the dog, he was alone now and quite confused.

"Grandmother, and I will always think of you as that, you are the only one who cared for me. You tried to prepare me for... I'm still not sure. You left me a book that *rewrites* itself? My *coming* hardships? And all this money?" He wished she were here to answer his questions. Removing the items one at a time, he took his time to examine each one closely lest he miss some hidden property or function. Everything was suspect now.

There was the book mentioned in the letter. It smelled old and musty and a bit like copper. The leather binding was slightly frayed and embossed with an intricate pattern of symbols and shapes. Held closed with a strap and metal clasp assembly, there was no obvious way to open it, no key or lever. He searched the box for something to use and had nearly given up when, by chance, he touched the metal clasp. Warm against his finger, it grew even warmer as he continued to press it. He was startled when it popped open.

Tucked into a pocket on the front cover was a tiny golden blade. It was very sharp for something so small, but there was no indication of its purpose. Above the pocket were three symbols carved into the cover. The pages of the book were blank. Yellowed and thicker than any ordinary pages of a book, Jake could see that they were not made of paper. Tiny lines emanated from the center of the page to the outer edges, and except for the pattern they made, there was nothing else.

After flipping through the entire volume and finding nothing at all written there, he decided look at it again later. He closed it, and touching the end of the clasp to the book, it snapped into place with a click. With a certain amount of awe, he set it aside to examine the rest of the contents of the box. There were two passports, two driver's licenses, and debit cards with two different names, Jacob Rowan and Jake Rune. The passports and licenses displayed recent photographs, and he recognized them from the strip of photos he had taken at the arcade on the boardwalk earlier that year.

A golden necklace with something that looked like an ancient amulet was of particular interest. He placed it around his neck, and held the tiny amulet in his hand. It looked valuable, but feminine, and he couldn't picture himself wearing it anywhere. Then he dropped it inside of his shirt. He could have sworn it was making some kind of buzzing sound. Other than that, nothing magical happened. He lifted it from around his neck and placed it back inside the box.

There was a sticky note attached to the debit cards that read, "Pin Number 06660." He made a mental note and pulled out his wallet to insert the cards. *That is an easy one to remember. I should probably deposit some of this cash into that account.* Except for his school ID and the burger joint loyalty card, his wallet had been empty until now. He slid the cards in the vacant slots and put it back in his pocket.

At the very bottom of the box, the scroll that had belonged to his great grandfather looked like old leather. It was bound tightly with a piece of thin silk cord, secured with sealing wax and an impression of a symbol unlike anything he had ever seen.

It was evident to Jake that he could not simply tuck these items in his pocket and carry them out of the bank. He would need some kind of bag. Perhaps the woman who had been helping him would have something he could use. Before calling her in, he placed everything back in the box and closed the lid.

"Excuse me, ma'am." He stuck his head out the vault door and addressed her.

"Yes? Is there something I can help you with?" She had just finished some business with another customer, so she excused herself and crossed the floor to him.

"I was wondering if you might have some kind of bag I could use to put a few things in."

"Of course, Mr. Rune. We offer a tote bag as a premium to open a new account, but since you are such an important client here, you can have one or as many as you like. Please excuse me a moment while I get them for you."

"Sure, I'll be right here, but I only need one."

He went back into the vault to wait, his mind reeling with all he had discovered so far. Overwhelmed as he was, he realized there was so much about his life that he had never known. He had been raised to believe that he was just another guy. He was at the beginning of life. He'd been an honor student, recently graduated from high school along with the rest of his class, and he was still trying to decide if he should attend college.

"Wait a minute… school."

Some things about his youth were beginning to make sense. During his sophomore year, a counselor had told him that he could earn a full scholarship to several universities if he was able to keep his grade average high enough. However, when he had spoken to his grandmother about it, her response had been, "I am so proud of your accomplishments, Jake, but college won't teach you what you need to be successful. We have bigger plans for you after graduation." Bigger plans indeed!

"Mr. Rune, excuse me, I have your bag here." The woman stood at the door with three bags, each a different color, red, blue and black.

"I'll take the black one, thank you." She handed him the bag and smiled. He took the bag and walked back to the table.

Jake unzipped the bag, removed some rolled up paper and stuffed it in the small trashcan near the table. He placed four stacks of hundred dollar bills in the bag before adding the book and the scroll. He added the professor's business card to his growing wallet. Zipping the bag, he put everything else back into the box and closed the lid. Through the doorway he called, "I'm finished now."

The woman rose from her desk and came into the vault. "Everything was satisfactory?" she asked as she slid the safe deposit box back into place. She locked it with both keys and handed his key back to him.

"Oh sure, wonderful." he said, as she walked him to the door.

"Thank you for your business, Mr. Rune. We hope to see you again soon." She offered her hand to him and he shook it.

"I'll be back, for sure."

"Have a nice day then." She smiled and went back to her desk as he left the bank.

TWO

Back outside in the sunlight, he looked around for Pete who was nowhere to be seen. He felt panicked until he saw the dog emerge from behind some bushes.

"Was there some trouble?"

Pete shook some leaves from his fur. "Cops, two of them cruised past here very slowly. They were about to spot me. No leash, no tags. Bad news, I'm guessing."

"Well, we'll just have to take care of that."

"Just how do you propose we do that? I don't know much about human things, but I know that almost everything in your world requires money." The dog followed Jake as he turned to walk down the sidewalk.

"We have the money now, Pete. We are going to get you your tags, a new collar and a leash. You'll have to get your shots too, and then we're good to go. I think we should check into registering you as a service dog though. They let service dogs go places where ordinary dogs like you can't go." He turned the corner at the next intersection.

"Why does it sound like those shot things are going to be bad for me, and what, pray tell, is a service dog?" Pete was trotting along next to him opposite of the side where he carried the bag. "And… what is that awful smell?"

"A service dog helps the blind to walk around more freely, or someone who is disabled to manage their life with less assistance. So, what smell are you talking about?" He had to dodge to keep from crashing against a trashcan while turning to talk to the dog.

"What are you carrying in that bag, Jake?" Pete switched sides so he could sniff at the bag. "I feel fairly certain there's something dead in there."

"Yeah, it's a squirrel." He allowed a moment for the joke to hit the dog, but there was no indication that he understood it was meant to be funny.

"Obviously, I wouldn't be carrying something dead around in a bag." Jake laughed. "I've got some money, an old book and a scroll. The writing on the scroll looks like the same writing that is now burned into my body." He made a quick exit from the street into an alley and, as soon as they were out of view, he set the bag on the ground.

"Come here." He squatted and unzipped the bag so the dog could see inside.

"Wow. Is that real money? I don't know a lot about such things, but it looks like a lot." Pete stuck his whole head into the bag before Jake could stop him. When he came up for air, he was holding the scroll by one corner, clutching it between his clenched teeth.

"Here it is." He hissed without dropping the rolled document.

"Yeah, it's a scroll. It appears to be written on leather or sheepskin, maybe. Clearly, whatever animal it was taken from died before they took its skin. That's probably what you smell, right?"

The dog dropped the scroll back into the bag and looked the boy in the eyes. "No cow or sheep died to make that scroll, Jake. That's human skin."

Suddenly, Jake went pale. He felt sick to his stomach. Fighting back the urge to vomit, he sat down on the old paving stones of the alley and zipped the bag shut.

"Damn, the letter said the scroll belonged to my great grandfather. Do you think that means that it's his... skin?"

"I didn't know your great grandfather, but I'm guessing he left you a memento." Pete licked his chops. He dared not admit that, despite the terrible odor, it tasted kind of like bacon.

"This is no time for jokes," he sniped at the dog. "If this is the skin from his back..." He raised his arm and put his hand beneath his collar, rubbing his neck. "Is this why the demons are attacking me? To get the skin off my back?"

"I'm not so sure that it's the only reason, but it's probably something like that."

"I think we should get off the street. Let's find a hotel. I need time to think, and I'm almost too tired to do it right now." Jake stood up and started walking again.

"So, where are we headed?" The dog followed at his heels.

"I think there's a Hometown Inn a few blocks from here. It'll give us a chance to rest and sort things out."

"I think it's going to take more than a nap to sort this out." Pete didn't sound very optimistic.

"You don't say." Jake turned left at the next corner and continued toward the hotel.

Three

Jake woke from a dead sleep. He thought he had heard screaming. He sat up and looked around the hotel suite, rubbing his eyes.

"Did you hear that?" he asked Pete. The dog was sprawled out on the love seat.

"Hear what? All I heard was you talking in your sleep. By the way, who is Jeremy, and what's the big deal with the cookies?"

"Cookies? I was talking in my sleep?"

Pete yawned, "Yes, you certainly were. You said something like, if Jeremy didn't drop the cookies, you were going to do something to him. I didn't quite get that part. You mumbled something, and then you sat up. I have to say, it was pretty strange."

"I don't know what was happening, I was out of it. You didn't hear anyone screaming?" Jake stretched and got out of the bed. He crossed the floor to the bathroom in five steps.

Pete jumped off the small sofa and followed him. "None whatsoever. Wow! That's really... are you a fireman or something?"

Jake was midstream and turned his back to the dog, "Damn, dog! How about a little privacy here."

"Sorry, I don't really think about things like privacy. Where I come from, and certainly in this world, as a dog there's no such thing. Tell me now, what are we going to do? What's your plan?"

Jake went to the nightstand by the bed. "Help me find a phonebook."

"What's a phonebook?"

"Never mind." He expected more from one so old.

He checked the drawer and then the dresser, but there was nothing. Picking up the phone, he dialed '0' for the front desk.

"This is Barb. How may I help you?"

"Yeah, I was wondering, do you have a phonebook I can use?"

"Feel free to use the Wi-Fi. It's complimentary." She snapped.

"I would if I had a computer with me. It sure would be a big help if you could send a Yellow Pages book up to room 412." Jake waited.

"Please hold."

After a few minutes, she came back to the phone. "Yes, sir. I have it. I'm sending it up right now."

"Thanks." Jake hung up the phone.

"Two things we do today. First, get your shots and make you legal. Then we need to get me an awesome new smart phone."

"Which comes first then, me or the phone?"

"You do. I don't want any more hassles because of your obvious canine appearance and lack of legal accessories."

"Yeah, sure, I get it. It's always the dog's fault."

"I'm sorry. Neither of us chose to be in our current situation. I know I didn't."

"I'm just not used to all the rules that humans impose on each other. I'll get over it. So this service dog thing you mentioned earlier, will we get that too?"

"I need to get more information on it. If we can make it happen, our life will be a lot easier."

Pete snorted. "Believe me Jake, there is nothing about this life that is going to be easy."

FOUR

The veterinarian's office was just a taxi ride away, and it wasn't long before they were sitting in the waiting room. Jake was filling out all the papers that were needed to see the doctor and get the shots the dog needed. When he came to a question he couldn't answer, he would whisper to Pete. The dog would growl or bark the answer softly.

He was sporting a new collar and leash that they had picked up on the way. It turned out, it was a requirement for seeing the vet, and it gave the impression that Jake had taken his responsibility as a dog owner seriously. To all concerned, it would appear that he had control of the animal. Truth be told, no one had control over Pete.

"How old are you?" he whispered.

"How would I know? I don't do well with time measurement."

"I'm going to put eight years old then. Have you had any shots before?" Jake whispered.

"Is that important? We are here to do that now, right?"

"It's one of the questions on the form. Do you remember going to a vet, maybe when you were a puppy?"

"I wasn't using this body when it was a youngling either. I tried that once, way too messy. You have no idea what it's like to have your gut full of pinworms. Believe me, it isn't pretty. Been there, done that."

Pete stood up as a woman with a Doberman entered the office. He barked a couple of times and sat back down. Before the woman had time to take a seat, her dog lay on the floor trying not to make eye contact with him or Jake.

"I didn't understand that. What did you say?" Jake nodded toward the other dog, now hiding its head behind the woman's leg.

"You didn't understand because you don't speak *Dog*. I just told it to stay back or I would rip its heart out," Pete replied matter-of-factly.

"Excuse me, did your dog just say something?" The woman looked at him with her head cocked exactly as her dog had done when Pete had spoken to him.

"Uh… no." Embarrassed, Jake was saved from having to respond when the vet called, "Pete Rune."

As they waited in the examination room, Pete appeared increasingly nervous. When Jake asked him what was wrong, he whined, "Screaming, I can hear it from the other room."

Jake reached down and gave the dog a reassuring pat. "Don't worry, I got your back."

Following Pete's exam and blood tests, the doctor gave him his shots. "See, that wasn't so bad." Jake patted the dog's head and scratched his ear as Pete offered a longsuffering sigh.

Jake thanked the vet and went to the front desk to pay his bill. Before leaving, he asked if they knew what was needed to register Pete as a service dog. The information he received seemed simple enough, and the doctor scribbled on a piece of paper the name of a store that sold the supplies and ID tags.

He shoved the address in his pocket while he fastened Pete's new tags on his collar. When all was in order, they hit the street again. This time, the dog was totally legit. No more hiding from the police.

FIVE

While Jake waited at the counter to check out his new smart phone, Pete sat outside tied to a post. His leg and hip ached from the injections, and he felt somewhat queasy. He hoped they would take a break after this stop and get something to eat to settle his stomach. Through the window, he could see the clerk in the store showing Jake the various functions of his new phone. It was half an hour later when he came out of the store smiling.

"I never had my own phone before, and I sure never expected to get one like this!" He held it up to show the dog, but Pete expressed no interest.

"Look, it does everything. I can even access the web with it."

"Great, I'm glad you love it. Why you would want access to a spider's web does not make sense to me. Can we get something to eat now?" His stomach was rumbling. "Why don't you ask your shiny new phone where we might find the closest dog-friendly restaurant?"

Jake fiddled with his phone as they walked. "The vet told me that it would not be difficult to get your service dog gear. Then we can go anywhere, any restaurant, even on a plane. In fact, if we had it already, you would have been able to go into the phone store with me."

"Sounds wonderful, I really feel like I missed something. Any word on the food?"

"Give me a minute, this thing is more confusing than I expected."

More than once he had a close call, first nearly colliding into a woman walking the other way, and then dodging a light pole before a near miss with a tree. Pete dutifully followed beside him tethered by the leash.

"Something's wrong, Jake, and it's more than my stomach."

The dog was dragging behind him now, but Jake had been so distracted that he hadn't really paid attention to what he was saying. Suddenly Pete refused to go any further. The leash pulled from his hand as Jake was jerked backward.

Ahead, three homeless men were closing in on them. Jake kept his eyes riveted on their movements, while Pete watched two other suspicious looking characters slowly creeping up from behind them.

"Looks like there are five of them," he growled. "We are about to deal with the stink squad. I could smell those homeless guys a block away. It's pretty bad when the stench covers the scent of a demon."

"You couldn't warn me that we were about to walk into a trap, why? Because they don't bathe?" Jake's mind was racing as he tried to decide what his next move should be.

Pete turned to face the two men coming up behind them. "I sensed something in the air, but I had no way to know there would be so many. These guys are drones. They don't emit the vibrations or the odor as strong as the others do," he growled. "Uh, there is something I haven't told you yet."

"What's that?"

"I know you don't want to hear this, but there are going to be times when you'll have to kill a human host. If you don't, they will overrun you and tear you apart. It's purely self-defense, Jake. Don't hesitate if it comes down to it, or this party will be over."

"Thanks for the warning."

Jake dropped the bag he was carrying. He tried to recall his training as he prepared for the attack. The three men in front of him were each taking a turn at challenging him, alternately lunging a foot or so forward, then retreating.

Pete had taken on his fighting stance as any dog would. The hair on his back was sticking straight up, and he bared his teeth to warn any who dared to approach that they were at risk of losing a body part if they came any closer.

"Back off, or you will be dispatched," he warned the prospective attackers.

"Dispatched," Jake laughed. "You are a real word slinger." His heart was thumping as his adrenaline surged. In a flash, his mind carried him back several years to his training in the neighborhood warehouse that doubled as a martial arts studio.

***

Four of Jake's classmates closed in on him as his middle-aged instructor stood off to the side. "Remember, Jake, your eyes will deceive you. By the time you are able to focus, your opponents will have taken you down. You must sense them, anticipate their moves and think with their mind. A flock of birds moves as one because there is a leader. The moment the leader tires, another moves into position. Be that leader, Jake. Move into position and drive your opponents to the ground with their own energy. Lead them into the strike zone, and you will rarely be defeated."

***

Jake flashed again to the present just in time. The first assailant was making his move. He reached to take hold of the man's arm, and then using the forward momentum, drove him into the man coming from behind, sending both of them sprawling onto the concrete.

The next attack came from the left. The assailant tried to get his arm around Jake's neck, but the boy was swift to grab his shoulder, turn him sideways and land a thrusting kick to the kneecap. A loud "Kkkrrrraaack!" let Jake know that the leg had broken, folding backward as the man crumbled to the ground moaning.

As the first two attackers scrambled to regain their footing, Jake twirled on the next one who was coming at him from the right. Punching him full force in the solar plexus, he brought his knee up into the man's groin, causing him to fall forward onto his knees as he held his crotch and gasped for air.

The last man, who had circled around waiting for his opportunity, was now coming from behind. Jake could see him out of the corner of his eye and turned to grab hold of his wrist. As the attacker lunged forward, Jake stepped to the side, twisted his arm and flipped the man completely over. Slamming into the sidewalk, he lay stunned by the impact.

Pete was amazed at the boy's skills. He watched in awe, as Jake let loose on these hopeless, possessed bastards. However, it was time for him to step in. Zeroing in on one of the men rising up from the sidewalk, he let out a roar and lunged at the would-be assailant's throat, knocking him back, and clamped his jaws around the protrusion of the man's Adam's apple.

Pete stood on all fours pinning him down before launching away, tearing out the man's throat as he went. Desperately clutching at the open wound, jets of blood spurted with the rhythm of the dying man's pulse from between his fingers. He thrashed on his back on the concrete.

Jake had heard Pete roaring behind him, and something told him that one of his adversaries would no longer be a threat. That left one able-bodied combatant. He had pushed himself up from the sidewalk and was now more determined than ever to complete his mission. Circling Jake, he stepped over his fallen comrade all the while maintaining eye contact with his target. When he finally made his move, he lunged at Jake with a shrill, high-pitched scream.

"Enough of this!" Jake bellowed, grabbing the man by the shirt and smacking him on the forehead with his open palm. It happened so quickly that the demon inside the man had no chance to respond before it split from his body.

"You can't do this!" The evil creature, spat out, its vile breath nearly knocking Jake over.

"On the contrary, I just did." Jake smiled as he grabbed the demon and pulled it completely out. Twisting and thrashing about, it snapped at Jake with its mouth full of sharp teeth.

Dragging the beast along, Jake smacked each of the others who were attempting to get back on their feet and ripped the shrieking demons from their bodies. One by one they dropped, unconscious to the ground.

The last of the assailants was lying on the sidewalk in the final throes of death and was no longer a threat. His comrades, freed from the control of their hosts, lie scattered about. Jake kept a firm grip on the four squirming entities as he forced them to the ground. Holding them there with his foot, he recited the words he now knew by heart. The demons howled in agony until the last word was spoken, and Jake lifted his foot to allow their burning ashes to drift away.

"Come on, let's get out of here." Pete looked around at the five bodies strewn on the ground and began trotting in the direction they had been heading before the attack.

"What about these guys?" Jake was concerned. "Four of them will be okay, but the dead guy? Shouldn't I get the demon out of him?"

He stared at the man lying in his own blood sprayed over the sidewalk. "I didn't think it would get this bad. The cops will be looking for us."

"This is nothing, my friend. Eventually we may face hordes of them. I've seen it before. As far as the dead guy is concerned, the controlling spirit left its host as the body died. I felt it fly past me as it went. When the others wake up, they're not going to remember anything, so if the police show up, I'm sure they will make up some kind of story."

"Come on, Jake," he continued. "It's not our problem. These guys were rejects of society. No one will be looking for them, I can assure you." Pete looked away and licked the blood from his jowls.

Jake stared again at the bodies on the ground. Pete tried to offer an apology. "I'm sorry, Jake, about the dead guy. Perhaps I over-reacted. I'll try harder to control myself next time. I just didn't want them getting the best of you."

"Okay, okay, I'm sure you did what you felt you had to do. I'm not about to hold it against you. It's good to know you've got my back. Come on, we'd better get out of here." He grabbed Pete's leash and pulled him in the direction of their destination. "Hurry."

They ran for several blocks until Jake figured they were far enough from the scene to rest. He stopped to catch his breath, kneeling beside the dog.

"You know, we've been attacked three times in the last twenty four hours. I'm getting tired of it. We didn't have a chance to run from those guys. They boxed us in." Jake leaned against Pete, petting him as he tried to compose himself.

"Uh, thanks, Jake. I'm sure the dog I'm living in loved that kind of attention before I moved in. Sorry, it doesn't do much for me. I hope you don't expect me to lick your hand."

Jake blushed and gave the dog a friendly shove. "No, no hand licking. I was probably petting you as much for my own comfort as much as anything."

"Well then, whatever makes you feel better. You may continue." He pushed his head into Jake's hand for more.

SIX

Outside the restaurant, Jake noticed blood on Pete's legs. It appeared he had been sprayed during the attack.

"I need to clean you up before we go in. Wait here."

He hung the leash over a spike on the top of the fence that surrounded the restaurant patio and went inside. Moments later, he came out with some paper towels and cleaned the visible blood off the dog.

"That's better. Wait here while I wash my hands, and then we're going get something to eat."

With money no longer an issue, Pete was able to get the steak he had been longing for, and they sat outdoors without attracting any undue attention. When he had finished eating, Jake reached into his bag and pulled out the ancient leather bound book. He opened it up and looked through the blank pages, wondering what good it could be. Pulling out his wallet, he retrieved the business card that his grandmother had left him. "I think it's time to call this guy."

The card was nothing fancy, just a regular business card with the contact information for Ben Cramer, Ph.D., Professor of Ancient Languages and Cultures, NYU/UC Berkeley. The phone number was local. Jake dialed and waited for an answer.

"Hello, this is Cramer," came the deep voice on the other end. "You better have a good reason to interrupt my lunch."

Intimidated by that statement, Jake apologized. "I'm sorry. Should I call back later?"

"It depends. Who is this?"

Jake could hear the irritation in the man's voice. "Well, I'm calling because my grandmother left me a business card of yours. She said you would be able to help me. My name is Jake Row... Rune, Jacob Rune." Jake thought he heard something crashing in the background on the other end of the line. "Hello?"

"I... I didn't think she was serious when she came to me with that story," he mumbled. "Jacob Rune? Jake? Your grandmother contacted me several years ago. She... she said that on the day I would hear from you... it would be the most important day of my career. I remember her saying it like it was yesterday." The professor had gone from annoyed to enthusiastic in mere seconds.

At first, Jake had been caught off guard by his tone, but he could certainly understand the man's confusion. "She told me you would be able to help me figure out some things, and after what's been happening, I hope she was right."

"Indeed, Jake. I think we should meet as soon as possible. Where are you calling from?"

"I'm at a restaurant... um..." He looked around for a street sign.

"Look, I'm going to cancel my afternoon classes. I want you to meet me at my house as soon as you leave there. I'm headed home right now. Do you have my address?"

"No, sir. It isn't on your card."

"I have your number. I'll send it to you in a text message. You can receive a text, can't you?"

"I don't know, I guess so." Jake looked at his phone to see if he could tell how to receive a text.

"I'll send it now. Hang up. If you don't get it, call me back right away. Otherwise, I will see you when you get there. Oh, and thank you for calling, Jake. This is very exciting indeed."

"What did he say?" Pete was licking the last of the mashed potatoes from his plate.

"He wants to meet us right away. Are you about finished?"

"No dessert? Look, I cleaned my plate." The dog looked up from the shiny dish.

Jake was trying to put the phone back in his pocket when suddenly, it buzzed with the text message containing the professor's address. Jake squinted at the phone to read it. "Dessert? You want *dessert* now?"

"Sure, don't you eat dessert?" Pete looked up at him, with one of those *how-can-you-say-no-to-this-face* looks.

"Well, sure, I like desserts. I was just surprised that you would want it. You know, being a..."

"What, being a dog? You need to get past this dog thing, buddy. What do they say? Don't judge a book by the skin it's covered in? Anyway, I like sweets."

"So, if I were going to order your dessert, what would I be asking for?"

"Vanilla ice cream, no doubt about it."

"Vanilla? Why not chocolate? My favorite is chocolate."

"From what I've heard, chocolate is poison to dogs, and unless you have a *bring-the-dog-who-ate-chocolate-back-to life-spell* in that bag, I won't be trying it anytime soon."

Jake laughed at the sarcasm. "Not that I know of, but hey, there could be one in the book for all I know. That's why we're going to see the professor, to find out what we have here."

Just then, the waitress came back. She looked from Jake's empty plate to Pete's shiny clean plate and asked the million-dollar question. "Looks like you boys were hungry. Can I get you anything else then?"

There was some suspense as the dog leaned forward and licked Jake's hand. "Looks like somebody wants dessert today." She smiled.

"No, not today, thanks. Just the check, please. We have to be somewhere." He glared at Pete, giving him a *don't-you-dare-ask for-ice-cream* kind of look. As she walked away, he couldn't help but ask, "What was with the hand licking, man? Jeez, that was weird. You said you weren't going to do that."

"What, are you upset that the waitress noticed me?" Pete grinned as though he had just won some kind of a bet.

"No, it's not that. You're acting like a dog. A dog, a real dog would do something like that, but…"

"It was a ploy, obviously it didn't work. Listen, Jake, sometimes you just *have to* run with the skin you're in."

"Well, imagine yourself in a human skin then."

"You would rather I was a human licking your hand?"

"Oh, geez. Never mind." Just then, the waitress came with the check and a small dish of chocolate ice cream. Jake handed her a couple of twenties and got up to leave.

"The ice cream is on the house. Do you need change, sir?" she asked.

'No, keep it." He waved her off, and she winked at Pete before walking away.

"Did you tell her to bring that?" he gave Pete the look.

"Well, I thought really hard about ice cream. Evidently, I neglected to think vanilla."

"Serves you right. Do you want me to wait while you eat it and slip into a coma, or are you ready to go?'

The dog picked its leash up with its teeth and shoved it into the boy's hand. "Let's get going, smart ass."

SEVEN

A twenty-minute taxi ride set them at the doorstep of Professor Cramer's brick townhouse. When they got to the door, it swung open wide and a man in his late forties was standing in the entryway. "You must be Jack then?" He held his hand out.

Jake wasn't much for shaking hands, but he did so anyway. "And you must be Professor Creamer?" he joked and shook the man's beefy hand.

"Ah, that's Cramer." He corrected the young man in his best professorial tone.

"Yeah, I know, and I'm *Jake*." He smiled as the man moved to the side to let them in. He nodded toward the dog. "And this is Pete."

The professor's face tinged red with embarrassment. "I see. Sorry about that, Jake. Come on in and have a seat. I'm guessing we have a lot to talk about."

He led his two guests into a small living room area and through another doorway to the library. Jake was immediately impressed.

"I've never seen so many books in one place outside of a public library or a bookstore. This is pretty awesome." He was checking out the bookshelves lining every wall from the floor to ceiling, and every inch was crammed full of books. He noticed that some were very old and beautifully bound in leather.

In the center of the room was a large desk stacked high with more books and papers. The only other object there was a human skull. Jake pointed at it. "Is that a real skull?"

"That's what they told me when they gave it to me. It sure looks real, doesn't it? Supposedly, it belonged to the shaman of a mysterious nomadic African tribe."

Pete had been walking around sniffing at whatever he could reach until now. He couldn't understand the attraction of things such as books. Why would anyone want to spend so much time sitting in one place, looking at some dusty book, when the whole world was waiting just outside the door?

When the subject of the skull came up, he couldn't resist checking it out. He stepped forward and got up on his hind legs, setting his front paws on one of the only clear spaces left on the side of the desk. He smelled the skull.

"It's a fake," he proclaimed casually. "I can smell traces of plastic."

The professor had been taken by surprise when the dog got up and sniffed around his desk. "I don't mean to be short with you, Jake, but please control your dog. I have a lot of valuable…"

"It's a fake," Jake said matter-of-factly.

"What?" The man was surprised at his comment.

"The skull. Pete said it's a fake, made of some kind of plastic."

Jake grabbed Pete's collar and pulled him away from the desk. He shrugged at the dog apologetically. "Sorry, but I don't need the trouble if you make a mess."

The dog growled, "You don't have to get rough. I respond to simple commands."

The professor was astonished. "What did he say that time?"

"He said that he was being careful and to stop worrying."

"You *talk* to the dog." The look on the man's face was priceless.

"Yeah. Weird, huh?" Jake shrugged his shoulders. "But, there are stranger things than that happening, professor."

"Call me Ben, please. Maybe we should start at the beginning. Please, have a seat." He was intrigued. He would need as much information about the situation as he could get. He motioned Jake to sit in the big leather chair in front of the desk and then took his seat behind it. "Let me tell you what I know about *you* before you begin."

"Several years ago, a woman, your grandmother I suppose, came to me with a proposition. She said there would come a day when I would meet you…" He thought for a moment. "She said our meeting would be something very special that could change my life. She asked me to promise that, when the day arrived, I would help you. At the time, I thought she was just a crazy old woman. I said yes, I would help you, mostly so she would leave me alone. I gave her my business card and told her to call me when the day came."

He shifted in his seat, "That's all I know, really. How is your grandmother, by the way?"

"My grandmother was murdered a couple of nights ago, on my birthday." Jake's voice was calm, but his face showed signs that he was taking it harder than he let on.

"I'm so sorry. I didn't know…"

"I'm sure the news has not reported it. They killed her and everyone with her that night."

"Who did?"

"Demons, as far as I know. Pete called them huskers. Whatever they are, I know it was something evil. They've been trying to kill me ever since. First, it was a cop, then my girlfriend's mother and sister. Well, it wasn't actually *them*, but the demons inside them. Then, on the way here, a gang of homeless guys came out of nowhere."

Ben figured the boy must be confused. It was understandable since he was still trying to recover from the death of his grandmother. However, the professor couldn't help feeling skeptical about the boy's story. It was disconcerting. Here was a strange kid in his house, calmly telling him how his grandmother had been killed by demons, and then relating how other people, possessed by something evil, had attacked him. Had he been a fool to invite him in? Should he have made the dog stay outside?

"What makes you *think* it was demons, son?"

"I've seen them, horrible looking things. I don't know what else they could be." Jake was feeling desperate. "You don't believe me, do you? I guess the only way I can prove anything to you is to show you these."

He held his hands up to show the markings on his palms to the man. "And that isn't all of it. Here, too." He stood and turned away, pulling his shirt up to reveal the writing on his back.

"Mother of God… this can't be happening!" Ben stared at Jake's back. "Are these tattoos?"

"No, but I'm not sure what they are. They appeared at midnight on my birthday. It was as though someone burned them into me. It hurt like hell"

"Do you mind if I take a closer look? I might need to touch your back, is that okay? I don't want to creep you out." He opened a drawer and pulled out a large magnifying glass.

"Sure, go ahead." Jake was definitely curious about the characters on his back. If the professor could give him some answers, that would be a good thing. It was why he was here anyway.

Ben stepped closer and held up the glass to examine the boy's back. He turned the lamp on his desk to shine directly on the letters, and moved in even closer for a better look.

"Damn, I need my glasses." He walked around to the other side of the desk and rummaged through the drawer. He came back with a pair of wire-rimmed glasses resting on the bridge of his nose. Taking hold of the bottom of Jake's shirt, he lifted it up further over his shoulders to reveal the first line of text. He held the magnifying glass up to it.

"You're right, Jake. These are definitely not tattoos. There is no sign of scarring and the edges of these characters are well defined. There is no color bleeding at all. It's like someone ran you through a printer."

He pulled Jake's shirt down to cover his back again. "You can sit back down. I've sure as hell never seen anything like that before." He walked around the desk and sat back in his chair, removing his glasses and laying them on the desk.

"So, what does it say?" Pete grumbled from where he sat on the floor.

"Did the dog just say something? The rhythm of his growling makes it seem like he is speaking." He didn't wait for an answer. "I can't believe I just asked you that again." Clearly, he was embarrassed. He put his hand to his brow and massaged.

"He wants to know what's written on my back. He can't read. Don't worry, you'll get used to Pete."

Jake was as eager as the dog to know what message he was carrying around on his body.

"I'm sorry, I don't know yet. These runes aren't familiar to me. I'll have to research it." Ben leaned forward. "Wait a minute. You can really understand what the dog is saying. How do you do that, some kind of telepathy?"

"That night, on my birthday, he was following me down the street when the clock struck midnight. It was just before the change started. He was growling and barking, but it was just dog sounds until the bells of the church chimed twelve, and these marks were burned into me."

"After that, I could understand what he was saying. It's a good thing, too, or I'd probably be dead by now." He reached down and scratched Pete's head. "He told me he's here to help me. He says he's helped others before me as well."

Ben laughed, "Earlier today, I was working on lesson plans, bored out of my mind. I was even asking myself why I ever decided to follow the career path I did. Now, here you are. This is why. It changes everything."

"I know the feeling. It kind of sucks, though. Before this, I was thinking about where to go to college, you know, planning my life. Now, I'm trying to stay alive just walking down the street. To top it all off, I've lost everything and every one that mattered to me, except for … shit! I haven't called Maire to see if everything is okay at her house!"

"Maire?" The professor was genuinely interested. Another character was being introduced to this crazy scenario.

"My girlfriend, I should call her. Do you mind if I step into the other room for a minute to call her?"

"Sure. Pete and I will do some research while we wait, but before you go, let me take a picture of your back. I need a point of reference to work from." He took his phone from his pocket. Jake stood and turned, pulling up his shirt. Ben took three shots with the camera on his phone.

"That should do it," he said, reviewing the pictures. "Please, make your call." He waved Jake on. "We'll be right here."

As Jake walked into the adjoining room, Ben was scrolling through the screens on his phone. "I know it's here somewhere." He scrolled through two screens of icons until he found what he was looking for. "Ah-ha! Here we go."

Ben touched the icon on his screen and a whirring sound came from a printer in the corner of the room. Pete kept his eyes on the professor as he rose from his chair and walked to retrieve a hard copy of the photos he had taken. On his way back to the desk, he selected three books from different shelves of the bookcases.

"Here we go, Pete. I think the answer is here in these books. Let's see what we've got."

Pete stared at him with vacant eyes as he quietly barked out a couple of woofs. "Yeah, whatever."

EIGHT

In the small living room of the professor's home, Jake dialed Maire's number and sat down on the sofa. It rang three times before she answered.

"Jake! I was worried about you. Where have you been? Why didn't you call me before now?"

"Sorry, Maire. We stayed in the park until sunrise before going to the bank. You won't believe what was in that safe deposit box."

"I would believe anything after the things I saw you do. Are you gonna tell me or what?"

"For one, there was a lot of cash. I'm talking stacks of it. It has to be more than a hundred thousand dollars. There was also a very old book and a scroll with some writing that is like the words on my back. Maire, there were passports, credit cards, and all kinds of stuff. I even have a driver's license. Can you believe it? I never even took the test!"

"Are you serious? Passports and drivers licenses? A hundred thousand dollars? Wow, what are you gonna do with all that?"

"I'm not sure yet. There was a letter from Grandmother telling me to contact some professor, and I'm at his house right now. He's supposed to be able to tell me what the writing on my back says."

"So what *does* it say? Did he tell you?"

"No, not yet. He's researching it right now. Look, I've been worried… You haven't said how your mom and Lisa are doing? Are they okay?"

"Lisa is fine. In fact, she's doing great. You know how we used to argue about the smallest things? It's as if she's a different person, I mean, she's a *totally* different person."

"Mom isn't doing as well, though. Her shoulder is still hurting, and she went to see the doctor today. She thinks she fell down the steps, just as you thought she would, but she doesn't remember anything. The doctor thinks she may have hit her head. I was thinking when she told me that, *Like, yeah, Mom, probably when you smashed your way through the door!*" Maire let out a nervous laugh.

"Yeah, that was pretty awesome. Well, maybe not awesome, but you know what I mean. How did you explain that anyway?"

"I didn't even try. I told Dad I had been sleeping when all of a sudden my door exploded and woke me up!"

"He believed you?" Jake laughed.

"Yeah, but now he's freaked out. He looked through the whole house, spent hours on the web researching poltergeists, and even called some ghost hunter service for advice. I feel sorry for him, but there is no way I'm going to tell him the truth." She sighed, "He probably wouldn't believe it anyway."

"I know what you mean. I hate it when you tell the truth and people accuse you of lying." He had never experienced it at home, but at school, they didn't seem to trust anyone.

"Wait. Are you talking about me? I'm sorry about that, Jake, but..."

"No," he interrupted. "I wasn't talking about you. I understand that it's hard to take in all that's happening to me. I didn't believe it myself at first. It's all so strange."

"I know, right? So, I really miss you. When will I see you again?" He felt like telling her not to worry, it would all work out, but he couldn't be certain it *would* work out.

"I'm not sure yet. I need to find out what all this is about. It might take a while, Maire. I'll call you, okay?"

"'You'd better. Don't wait so long next time."

"Í won't, I promise."

"I love you, Jake. Please be careful."

"Yeah, you too."

As the call ended, Jake could hear the professor talking excitedly in the other room. He hurried in to see what it was all about and found Ben reading from one of his books. Pete was sitting in the chair across from him leaning forward as though trying to see the book for himself.

"So now you're talking to Pete?" He smiled.

"You know, I may not be able to understand what he's saying but I think I get the gist of it." He looked at Jake over the top of his glasses. "Wait until you hear what I have found."

"This guy has no idea what I am saying," Pete growled, "Watch this. Hey, funny man, you look stupid with those glasses hanging off your nose."

"Don't tell me what he said." Ben looked up from his book again. "He told you that we found an entire book on the language written on your back. Right?"

"Not exactly, but you're close." Jake made a face at Pete as he went on. "You found something about the words on my back?" Pete sighed, and rested his chin on the armrest.

"I most certainly did. I was concerned that I might have loaned it to someone, but here it is." He held up the book and turned it so Jake could see the pages. "Only one problem. It isn't complete. I'm going to have to try some other resources. You can stay here tonight if you want. I have cable. You can crash on the couch. It's up to you. I'll be working in here."

"Thanks, that's okay. I can afford a hotel."

"Jake, I think we should accept the offer. I've sniffed this place out, and it's safe for us, at least for now. We need to find out what we are up against as soon as possible." Pete looked at him with piercing eyes, but Jake needed little convincing.

"Pete says he wants to stay, so I guess we'll be here, at least for tonight anyway."

NINE

Shortly after three in the morning, Pete woke Jake from a dream. He poked at his charge with one of his paws. "Jake, wake up. Come on, he has it translated."

"Huh?" Jake sat up yawning.

"The mad professor translated the writing on your back. He just finished. Let's go!"

"What does it say?" Jake was still yawning as they walked to the library.

"No idea. He said it is for your ears only."

"There you are!" Ben was beaming. "The writing on your back is an extremely old language. It dates back to some time in the first century, just about two thousand years ago."

"So what does it say? You're killing me with the suspense!"

"I think you should sit down. You want some coffee?"

"No. Have you been awake all night?" Jake wiped the sleep out of his eyes.

"Yes, of course. This is so unbelievably intense. I wouldn't have been able to sleep if I'd tried. Back to the writing..." Ben sat down at the desk and picked up a notepad. "I'm just going to jump right into it."

"You are the last of the demon killers. There were six skins before you. You must find them so you can learn the words that must be spoken in order. The moment the last word is spoken, the gate of the cracked earth will open and the demons will be returned to the place from whence they have come. The book is both the map and key. Beware those who approach you, for they are the possessed. Quis

Nostrud Exerci Autem Erat Veniam." Ben looked up from his notes. "That's all that I have."

"Okay. So, now that you translated it, what does it mean?"

"I think it means you have some difficult work ahead, Jake," Pete weighed in. "You are the seventh and last in a family line spanning thousands of years. Those who came before you were also demon killers."

Pete paused to scratch at the rug on the floor before sitting down. "There's a story I have heard about your kind. I wasn't sure if it was true until now."

"If you knew more about this, Pete, why didn't you say something before? Tell me about it."

"What's he saying?" Ben was listening, but all he could hear was the unusual rhythm of barking and growling again. He had no idea what Pete was talking about.

"He knows more than he's been telling me," Jake grumbled. He looked back to the dog and waited. "Go ahead."

"I didn't bring it up before because it would have been pointless to tell you without proof. It's been said that a demon killer would appear every few generations, each one with a mission to send us back to hell. It has also been said that there would be seven of you, it is a magical number. It goes like this.

Six came before, the seventh scroll unrolled. He needs seven times the words and to remain alive to chant them.

Then there was some other stuff I can't remember except... *and the last of the line will be most powerful.* You are the end of the line, Jake. That is why they have made their plans for the Invert, to try and stop you."

"What is he saying?" Ben was leaning forward in his chair with great interest. Jake raised his hand to ask him to wait.

"Many will come against you. They desire to take your life. You must beware, Jake. One is coming who is more powerful than the all of others. The Invert desires to tear the skin from your back and steal the texts of your ancestors. Your purpose is to open the passage and send the demons back, while the Invert's purpose is to open the passage so those who remain in the realm of darkness might come through to overtake and rule your world." Pete was panting by the time he finished.

"Do you know who this *Invert* is?"

"Invert? Please, tell me what the hell he is saying. This is maddening! Speak English, dog!" Ben's face was turning red in the light of the desk lamp.

"He says there is someone or something out there that is the opposite of me. That person is supposed to kill me and open a door to the demon world so they can all come here. Is that right, Pete?"

The dog nodded as Ben burst out with, "Oh, shit! I've heard of that before. I thought it was mythology."

"It sounds all too real to me with everything that has happened the last couple of days. Right now, if someone told me a purple walrus the size of a battleship was about to fall from the sky, I think I would be looking for a safe place to hide." Jake chuckled nervously.

"Seriously though, I have a book here in my bag that is supposed to contain the answers to any questions I might have, along with a scroll of text written on the skin of my great grandfather."

Ben stared at him incredulously, "I can't believe you haven't told me this before now. Why didn't you say something?"

"I don't know. I guess I wanted to be sure that you knew what you were talking about before I let it out of the bag, so to speak. Hang on, let me get them." Jake headed off to the other room where he had left the bag next to the sofa.

"This is overwhelming. I think I need a drink." The professor opened the bottom drawer of his desk and pulled out a bottle of bourbon and a glass. He held the bottle out to the dog, "You want a swig?"

Pete cocked his head and replied, "That's right. Get drunk so you won't be of any use to anyone, silly man. And, don't you know that alcohol is bad for dogs. Are all human teachers really this stupid?"

Jake returned carrying the bag and set it on the desk. "Did I miss something?" he asked as he unzipped the bag.

"Oh no, Jake, I just asked Pete if he wanted a sip of bourbon. I have no idea what he said."

"What did you say, Pete?" Jake asked as he reached into the bag and pulled out the book. He released the latch and handed it to Ben across the desk.

The dog could not believe he was going to have to explain every utterance directed toward Ben. "I said, No thanks." With an audible sigh, he walked around the chair for a better view of the book.

TEN

Ben slowly turned the pages. "There is some writing on the inside of the cover, but the rest of the book is blank."

The professor studied the characters written there, and then looked at Jake with concern. "This is very strange. I don't think you're going to like it."

"What does it say?" Jake began to feel anxious.

Ben held up the small golden knife, "It says here you must provide the ink in order to read the book. You must cut yourself with this knife and allow your blood to drip onto the center of the page." He waited while Jake made a face.

"I have to bleed on the page? Do I have to slice it with that knife? Can't I just poke my finger with a pin and squeeze some out?" He held out his finger and squeezed it.

"We can try that. Yes, it might work." Ben opened his desk drawer and pulled out a needle. "I have no idea why I have one of these in here, but it looks like it will come in handy. Let me sterilize it." He pulled a lighter out of the drawer and held the flame under the needle for a few seconds. After allowing it to cool, he handed it to Jake. Poke your index finger, and squeeze some blood into the center of the page." He turned the book around and slid it across the desk in front of Jake.

Holding the needle tightly, Jake poked his index finger. "Ouch!" But, nothing came out when he squeezed it.

"Are you sure you poked it in far enough?" Ben asked. "Want me to do it for you? I'll be quick about it."

"No, I pushed it in deep. I should have gotten some blood."

Pete decided it was time to speak up again. "I believe it's healing before you can get any blood. I'm guessing that's why the knife is provided. You will have to cut yourself to get enough blood to fill the pages."

The thought of cutting himself did not sound appealing to Jake at all. He voiced his objection. "Are you freakin' kidding me? That's gonna hurt."

"What is?" Ben was fiddling with the small knife while he waited.

"Give me that blade." Jake reached for the knife as the professor handed it over.

"You're not going to…"

Jake cried out as he sliced his finger open and held it over the page of the book to allow a few drops to fall before the bleeding stopped. Jake and Ben watched in awe as the blood traveled throughout the veined pages, spreading out to reveal what was written there. As Ben turned them, the writing on each one began to appear.

"What does it say?" Pete wanted to know.

"I don't know, what do you think?" Jake looked at Ben

"Let me take a look." The professor pulled the book closer to get a better look. "Amazing. I need some time to research the language. It's not at all familiar to me." He flipped through the pages again, stopping to take a long look at one in particular. "There are maps here. Wow, guys, you should take a break while I investigate."

The professor studied the book for nearly half an hour before finally commenting. "I can understand some of it. There's something of a legend at the beginning. The rest of the book seems to be instructions, including places and names, and there are maps on several of the pages." He inhaled sharply. "Whoa, wait a minute!"

"What's wrong?" Jake leaned over the desk to try and see what Ben was looking at.

"I could swear the map I was just looking at changed, and I mean right before my eyes!" Beads of sweat broke out on his forehead.

"What do you mean, it changed?"

"At first, it looked like the map was showing a place in the Mediterranean, maybe Greece. See the coastline?" He held the book so Jake could see where he was pointing. "Then, the whole map seemed to shift on the page, like it was tracking something as it moved." Ben stared down at the page. "This is going to sound crazy, but it's like some kind of ancient GPS tracker. Look there! It just moved again."

"The book that rewrites itself…." Jake mumbled.

"Did you say the book that rewrites itself?"

"I was thinking of the letter from my grandmother. It said that the book is rewritten somehow as the conditions in the world change. I wasn't sure what that was supposed to mean, but this could be it." Jake sat back in the chair. "What do you think it's tracking?"

"I'm not sure. I'll have to translate the pages around the maps to see if it tells us anything." Ben turned the pages carefully, looking for answers.

"I am guessing that the maps are used to locate the scrolls." Pete volunteered.

"That makes sense." Jake was glad for Pete's insight.

"What makes sense? What are you two discussing?" Ben could hardly contain his excitement.

Pete continued, "Well, there were six demon killers before you. You have one scroll in the bag and one is still on your back, which means there are five others out there somewhere. Ask him how many maps are in the book."

"He wants to know how many maps are in the book." Jake inquired of Ben.

"Well, give me a minute and I'll count them again." Ben went to the beginning of the map section and started counting the maps. "There are five different maps and then a blank page."

Jake turned to Pete, "So you think the maps are the locations of the scrolls? If that's true, then all we have to do is use the maps to find them."

"Shit!" Ben set the book down. He picked up the bottle of bourbon and poured some into his glass. "The dog is right. There are six maps in total, but here's the kicker." He turned the book again so Jake could see. "This map, right here, shows where we are. Right here, this is my house!"

He pointed to a red blotch on the map, "This is YOU, Jake. The other mark that is almost on top of it must be the scroll in your bag."

Ben leaned back, setting the book on the desk again. "Jake, whatever you're involved in, it's so much bigger than your grandmother told me about years ago. I know I made a promise, but I don't know if I can do this."

Jake knew he would not be able to do it alone. He was greatly relieved when Pete cut in again. "Tell him he can do it. It's his destiny. We don't always choose our destiny, sometimes it chooses us."

Jake looked at Ben and repeated what the dog had told him. "Pete says this is your destiny, Ben. You don't have a choice. You're involved now."

The professor looked up from his desk and nodded. "I think he's right. I always felt that I was meant to do something more than teach, that there was some greater purpose for my life. And now, here it is." Pushing back his thinning hair, he finished his thought. "I only wish I had been more prepared."

Jake understood exactly. "I can second that emotion. I feel the same way."

ELEVEN

In a countryside chateau outside of Paris, one room was stained in tones of crimson and bloody flesh. Here a young woman, a dazzling beauty of feminine perfection, was coming into the fullness of her power and purpose in a ritualistic slaughter of thirteen servants of evil. Just as her counterpart across the ocean had been experiencing a life-altering transition into the Awareness, so was Seraphine. Unlike her invert, however, the young woman was fully aware of her mission.

Thirteen demons now in possession of her were of one purpose. However, they could not agree how they would accomplish it. Eventually, one of them would take control, absorbing all others in order to concentrate their power as one terrible entity. Each had become accustomed to the liberty of residing within their individual hosts. Now, they had to forgo that freedom in order to fulfill their mission. They would fight amongst themselves for the privilege of controlling this shapely human body and the fate of their brethren.

Seraphine sat quietly at the window for many hours as the battle for power was taking place within her. She seemed at peace, taking in the serenity of the garden behind the large home. At the beginning of her transition, Lob, who had been in control of forty legions in the past, felt entitled to hold the position of power within the Invert. Her arrogance proved foolish, and she was soon absorbed by the more powerful Argo who possessed the strength of a thousand legions.

The tug of war within Seraphine stretched on into the evening. As each succeeding entity was overcome, it melded into the formidable being that would empower the young woman. The vacant look in her eyes belied the ongoing battle. With the last two entities wrestling within her, she was but moments away from reaching the fullness of her transition.

Then it happened.

A rumble of thunder rolled across the countryside. To the villagers in the surrounding area, it seemed like any other storm on the horizon. They were completely unaware of the magnitude of what was about to transpire.

Seraphine stood in the center of the room. Her arms were outstretched as the iridescent blue of her eyes faded into lifeless platinum. The light surrounding her seemed to bend and shimmer like waves of heat as she absorbed the unseen energy within her.

A low vibration began to shake the house as another clap of thunder rolled across the fields. She spread her fingers as lightning flew from their tips and crashed through the ceiling. The blast tore a hole in its path through successive floors of the mansion and broke through the ceramic roofing tiles, peeling them off like scales. The dark energy bolted into the clouds above. The room was illuminated in hues of flickering blue as sparks licked at the walls, and at last passed through and out into the surrounding fields.

At once, every living thing, plants and trees alike, rose into the air. Around the chateau, even the green sod carrying the dirt within its roots hovered several feet above the scorched earth below. A passing flock of birds suddenly hung frozen in the sky in midflight.

Inside the structure, Seraphine was shaking violently as the energy pulsed through her until at last she screamed. It was a scream of such terrible volume and pitch that all of the windows immediately blew out. Mirrors, crystal, and chandeliers inside the chateau burst into a fine sparkling dust that floated around her until it matched the level of the hovering greenery outside.

For a moment, the beautiful Seraphine stood completely still, seemingly transformed into a statue of cold gray granite until she spoke a single phrase,

"Derman enlion kuchul."

Suddenly, everything dropped back into place. The dust settled within the chateau. The sod and foliage that had been ripped from the ground, fell back to the earth. Every living thing, whether on legs of flesh and bone or wings in the sky within a mile radius, fell dead to the ground.

The transition was complete. All within her had become one.

Seraphine was filled with the Awareness of her awesome power. No one would be her master, and she would have victory over any who would be foolish enough to try. Hers was a power of destruction and chaos unlike any this world had known before her. Should she survive the coming confrontation with the Demon Killer, she would bring a reign of hell to the earth and every living creature upon it.

RUNE

Episode III: Endeavor

ONE

"Did you see that flash?" Ben dropped the book in fear of what he might have done.

"Yeah, it came from inside the pages." Jake picked up the book and flipped through the leaves of ancient paper.

"Hey, remember the blank page I showed you when we were counting the maps? Well, there's a map there now." He turned the book so Ben could see the page.

Pete moved closer to view the page that Jake was now examining. It most certainly was a new map, but something about it was different from the others. Where each of the other maps had a red mark believed to signify the location of one of the scrolls, the new map had a black one. As the dog stared at the black mark, he finally realized what he was looking at.

"I believe we have just located the Invert," he growled in an ominous tone.

"What location is this map showing, and why do you think it's a different color?" The black spot seemed to hover nearly an inch above the page. "That dot isn't even on the page. It's floating."

"It doesn't look like it to me. Oh, hey, it's starting to fade. I need to take a picture so I can continue to study it."

Ben grabbed his phone from the desk and opened the camera app. He turned to the front of the book and snapped a shot of each page. "That should do it."

"Do you think you'll be able to translate it soon? We have a lot to figure out. I need to make some kind of plan before we start our journey to find the scrolls."

Jake took the book as Ben handed it back to him. Even as he watched, the text faded from the pages and was gone.

"Something's wrong with my camera." Ben turned the screen so Jake could see. "The pages are there, but there's no writing."

"Crap! The pages faded already. Are you sure none of your photos showed what was written there?"

"I don't think it's the camera. I think it's the blood." Pete had been watching as the pages faded and offered a guess, "The camera can't see it. As long as the blood is in the pages, the book is alive."

Jake stared down at the blank pages. "Soooooo... you think the page feeds on the blood? That's some crazy stuff!" His expression froze as his face went pale. "It's a vampire book?"

"Let's be realistic. Vampires don't exist, Jake. That's a myth." The look on the dog's face was priceless.

"Well, I would have said that about demons a week ago, so I'm not entirely convinced that they don't." He looked over at Ben who was silently watching them converse.

"Care to let me in on this scintillating conversation?" He looked perplexed and a little irked by the insider discussion.

"Pete says the book is a vampire because it lives on blood."

"I did not say it was a vam..." the dog hissed.

Ben cut in, "I knew something was strange about it. That explains why the camera didn't work. Just like when you can't see a vampire's reflection in a mirror."

"That's only in the movies. Besides, now he's saying that vampires don't exist."

"Yeah, like demons." Ben was checking the lens on his phone before wiping it with the tail of his shirt.

"Exactly! That's what I said. So what do we do now?" Jake wasn't sure he wanted to know the answer to his question.

Ben handed him the small knife. "You'll have to feed the damned thing again. We need to know what to do next."

"Why do I have to do it? It hurts like hell. You try it this time. You can probably get away with using the pin."

"I bet his blood doesn't work." Pete tossed out, but the humans paid him no attention.

"I think we should try your blood at least once. Go ahead, Ben."

The man hesitated for a moment or two before giving in. "Okay, I'll give it a shot. Maybe it will *talk out loud* with my blood!" He smiled at his small attempt at humor, but the joke had fallen flat.

He picked up the needle from the desk and heated it with his lighter. When it cooled, he shoved it into his finger, wincing as he pulled it out. "That hurts."

He held his finger above the page and squeezed until a very large drop of blood fell directly toward the center. Jake would have said that it fell in slow motion if he had been asked, but there was nothing slow in the way the page reacted. The drop of blood rolled quickly to the edge and splashed to the floor. Not a trace was left on the book, which immediately slammed shut, the clasp locking tight.

TWO

Seraphine stood in the wreckage of the room and surveyed the result of her newly found power. The furniture was smashed, the wallpaper shredded, and a crystalline dust covered everything except for her. Rather than stay there another minute, she headed for the door at the entrance to the mansion.

The heavy wood of the double doors swung effortlessly as she stepped through. She found her escorts waiting patiently on the front steps: two giant men ready to protect her, willing to sacrifice themselves if necessary. These servants from hell stood nearly seven feet tall, their rippling muscles bulging visibly beneath their well-tailored clothes.

They were built like a pair of professional wrestlers, the largest that had ever graced the ring. The bumps that covered every inch of their skin definitely set them apart from normal humans. They stepped up toward Seraphine and extended their huge arms to assist her descent.

"Frogoth and Betlamel, I am pleased to see you again. I trust your journey here was uneventful." She met their eyes directly, and they quickly deferred, looking down at the ground.

"Uh, huh…" Frogoth responded in a deep growl. "We come to serve you, mistress."

"Well then, we will leave here and begin our search for the foolish boy who thinks he can deny us our destiny. He will pay for his ignorance with his blood. I will savor every inch of his flesh as I rip it from his body and consume it myself."

The trio stepped from the stairs and walked to the circular driveway where a very large limousine awaited them. As they passed the withered landscape, she could appreciate the damage she had caused during her transformation. The ground was scorched everywhere as far as her eyes could see.

Trees and shrubs lay flattened, their leaves a dull brown. Small lifeless bodies of various kinds of birds peppered the area, and a stray cat that had been literally turned inside out lay on the paving stones between the woman and the car. She kicked her foot at it and sent it skidding across the drive before it finally tumbled into a pile of dead shrubbery.

"I believe things are going to be much different now. Wake up Paris, I am coming to devour you." The young woman laughed loudly as Betlamel opened the door for her and she climbed into the limo. "I'm going to enjoy this."

THREE

Jake had opened the skin on the palm of his hand with the small golden knife and allowed a large splotch of blood to fall on the page. He had considerable difficulties in getting the book open again after Ben's experiment and didn't want to go through that again. He hoped that drawing more blood would give them an extension of time to decipher the words.

"Something's wrong with the book now," Jake lamented as he observed the first few pages. "The letters look blurry."

"They look fine to me. What do you think, Pete?" Ben tilted the book so the dog could see.

"So now he's going to start talking to me with absolutely no understanding of how I respond? This is ridiculous." The dog looked at the book from where he was sitting, "The letters look perfectly clear to me."

Jake glanced back and forth between Pete and Ben as they spoke. Looking, back at the book again, he put his hand to his head.

"Wow, it's really bad now. Makes my head hurt looking at it. Do you have anything for a headache, Professor?"

Ben hesitated until Pete barked sharply then came around.

"Oh, sorry, I was just wondering why you could be seeing blurred letters… What did Pete say about it?"

"He said they look the same as always to him. I'm feeling queasy now."

"Right! Give me a minute."

He turned to exit the room and immediately began talking to himself. "Text looks fine to me and to the dog..."

Walking up the steps, he entered his bathroom and reached for the medicine cabinet.

"Soooo, if it looks the same to us, and looks blurry to Jake..."

He opened the medicine cabinet and grabbed a bottle of ibuprofen.

"Something is happening to him, maybe some kind of..."

Clutching the bottle of painkillers in his hand, he stumbled down the steps as fast as he could go.

"Jake!"

He hit the floor at the base of the steps and bounded toward the duo still occupied with the book.

"Jake, I think you are going through some kind of..."

"Change... I know. As soon as you left the room, I tried making out the letters again. This time the letters were clear, and I could read them, actually READ them!"

He turned the page. "It takes a lot of those characters to make a word doesn't it? So even though it looks like a lot of writing, it doesn't contain a lot of information."

Ben felt a twinge in his stomach. He had waited his entire career for an opportunity like this, and now it appeared that this boy and his dog would have no more use of him. In a weaker voice he asked, "So what does it say?"

"Are you okay, Ben? Your voice sounds strange." Jake was concerned. For a man that had seemed so excited when he entered the room, he now sounded somewhat sickly.

Ben cleared his throat. "No, no, I'm fine. What does it say?"

"He's not fine, Jake. Watch this." The dog turned to face Ben and began to speak in the hypnotic voice Jake had previously only heard him use on the night of his awakening. "What are you really thinking, oh Educated One?" His low growl swirled out from his canine lips.

Ben was silent at first, and then it was as if the floodgates had been opened to the maximum. "I'm afraid that since you can read the book, you won't need me anymore. It's just like all of my other relationships. As soon as the person gets what they want, they leave. No matter what I do, it's always over." Tears began to stream down his face as he continued, "I mean even in my freshman year of college when Carol asked me to take her to that concert…"

"Tell him to stop, Pete." Jake was perturbed with the dog for manipulating the man.

Pete was leaning forward and growling for the man to continue, but he sat back to respond to Jake.

"Come on, this story is getting good. I want to find out what happened with this Carol woman."

Ben was stuttering in the background and getting to some of the emotional details of the story when Jake finally shouted, "Enough!"

As the word left his lips, he felt a tingling sensation. The word seemed to spin and spiral as it echoed through the rooms of the old home. Pete sat gaping at Jake, and Ben seemed to come back to his senses.

"What just happened?"

"What do you remember?" Jake was genuinely concerned.

"I was headed upstairs to get something for a headache, but I don't have a headache. I feel fine."

"Oh. Well, I felt like I was getting a headache, but I'm okay now." Jake glared at the dog.

The professor set the bottle of pills he had been holding on the corner of the desk. "Did something happen while I was upstairs?"

Pete responded, "Sure it did, old man. Jake just discovered his voice."

He turned to Jake and flashed his familiar doggie grin. "I was wondering if you were going to be able to do that, and I have to admit, you're very good with it."

Ben looked to the boy for translation, but none was offered.

"What is it? I know he said something to answer my question, I can feel it. What did he say?"

"Ben, we need to talk." Jake pulled a chair over for the man. "Sit down, there's something I need to tell you."

FOUR

Seraphine sat in the back of the limo staring out the window as her henchmen navigated toward the nearest luxury hotel inside the Paris city limits. She did not blink as several voices spoke simultaneously in her head, although it was confusing to focus on any one in particular.

"One at a time, please," she spoke quietly to herself. The request brought forth an answer from a single voice.

"You need to find the Other and skin him alive before he begins searching for the scrolls."

The voice grated in her mind.

"If he succeeds at finding even one, he will grow stronger. We must eliminate him while he is still weak."

She answered the voice without making a sound. "What am I supposed to do? I have no idea where to begin. Who is this *Other* I am supposed be looking for? I have no idea where to begin."

"You must procure a document written in ink by the hand of a human. You will then be able to divine his location."

She had no clue where she would find such a thing.

"People don't use paper and ink to write anymore. They use computers and electronic documents. Even *I* know that people don't write much of anything by hand. That's the problem with you ancient ones, you refuse to change with the times and you…"

"To obtain the information you need, you must have a document written in ink. There is nothing to debate."

"Be careful of your tone, I am warning you. There are others equally as capable of guiding me. Your voice will be silenced permanently if you do not take care."

"My apologies, mistress. I exist only to serve you. Yet, for the time being, there must be paper and ink."

The voice in her head took a softer approach to avoid destruction.

"What about a newspaper? The words on its pages are written by humans and printed in ink on the paper. Will that do?"

"From your description, it would seem so. It is worth an attempt."

Concentrating, she silenced the voice for the moment. She leaned forward and pressed a button, opening the window between her and the front seat of the limo. "I need a newspaper, and I need it now," she ordered before pressing the button again to close the window.

The demonic thugs in the front seat looked at each other. In the passenger seat, Betlamel shrugged his shoulders. Frogoth pulled up to the first kiosk they came upon.

With the engine running, Betlamel stepped out of the car. He strode over to a stack of newspapers and grabbed one off the top without so much as a glance at the man in attendance. As he climbed back into the car, the outraged shop owner cursed at him.

"Hey, you need to pay for that!"

Running for the car, the old man grabbed at the door just as it slammed shut. The instant his fingers touched the metal handle, an intense pain erupted in his shoulder and traveled quickly down his arm. His hand immediately grew cold, and he could see that it had turned a dark shade of purple. Frightened, he released his grip on the door as the car revved and sped away. The spinning tires sprayed loose gravel into his face as he collapsed to the ground.

Inside the limo, Seraphine accepted the newspaper from her servant as he passed it through the window. The headline read "Cattle Drop Dead in Bizarre Incident." She smiled at how quickly the news of her power had spread. Perhaps she had misjudged the efficiency of the older methods of disseminating information.

"Now what?" she quizzed the voice in her head for instruction.

"Spread the paper on the floor before you."

She did as she was told and laid the paper at her feet. Before her mind even formed the question, her guide instructed her to wave the palm of her open hand slowly above the printed surface. As she did so, the ink on the pages began to move. The text seemed to merge into shapes.

"Once more, do it slower this time." The voice was firm.

As her hand completed the second pass, a map of the world was plainly visible.

"Again," ordered the voice.

The map zoomed to a location within the United States. A pulsating dot gave her the location of her enemy. He was in a place called Brooklyn, and the dot hovered over the exact location of Ben's house.

Again, she opened the window and barked orders at the pair in the front, "Contact our legion in New York. I have a mission for them. The exact location is..." She waved her hand over the paper again to extract the address.

FIVE

Jake sat at Ben's desk studying the pages of the book. He flipped them back and forth in an attempt to extract the full meaning of the words.

"There are two sets of numbers here and what appears to be a description of where I can find the first scroll, but it seems a little cryptic."

Jake rubbed the back of his neck. It was sore where the mark had been burned into it on the night of his birthday. It was warmer to the touch than the rest of his neck.

"The numbers, read them to me." Ben grabbed a pen and a sheet of paper from his desk. "Go ahead."

"Here we go, 33.8059 N. That's the first number, and 84.1454 W is the second. What is that supposed to mean? What's with the N and the W? Of course! That means..."

"They're map coordinates. Wait a sec." Ben moved to his computer and typed in the coordinates he had written on the paper. "Holy cow, Jake. It's a place called Stone Mountain. That's right outside Atlanta, Georgia. Does it say anything else?"

"Yes, here's the weird part. Check this out. It says, 'In the nostril of the beast traveler carved into the rock, you will find the skin that you seek.' What the heck does that mean?"

Ben looked at his computer monitor and rubbed his forehead.

"There's a famous carving on the face of the mountain. I think it means that inside the nostril of this horse, we'll find the scroll." He pointed at the picture on the screen. "That horse's head must be at least fifty feet high and the only one with a nostril open enough to safely hide a scroll."

Pete had been paying close attention. Alarmed, he gave voice to exactly the same concern that was tugging at Jake's mind.

"That's got to be very high off the ground. No way can I get to that. Not with these dog legs!"

"Yeah, I don't even know how *I'm* supposed to manage a feat like that," Jake answered.

"What, get inside that horse's nose?" Ben spoke up. "You can rappel down from the top of the mountain. It says here, there's an observation area on top."

"How did I know you were going to say that?" Jake swallowed hard. "I've had a lot of different types of training, but I'm not a mountain climber."

"That's the beauty of rappelling. You don't climb; you just start at the top and work your way to the ground. Judging from the size of this thing we're gonna need a heck of a lot of rope."

"I think we're going to need more than rope, Jake. I have a feeling this is going to be a challenge unlike any you've ever faced. Personally, I'd rather deal with a horde of demon-possessed homeless men than watch you hanging from a rock that high." Pete sounded genuinely concerned.

"I guess I don't have a choice, do I." He looked over at Ben who was intently listening to his side of the conversation with Pete. "How long does it take to get to Atlanta from here?"

"I don't know, maybe twelve hours or so. That is if we drive." Ben wondered if Jake was about to say his goodbyes.

"Do you have a car?"

"Well, I have an old Volkswagen van, but it still runs great. You could take that if you need it." His voice trailed off.

"Do you think you could teach me to drive?"

"You don't drive? I don't believe there is time for you to learn before you go, Jake. You need to get going as soon as poss..."

"No, I mean on the way. Do you think you could teach me on the way there?"

"You... you want me to go with you?"

Pete growled, "Jake, no. Did I say no? I meant, HELL NO!"

"Pete says he wants you to go. We need you." Jake grinned at the dog.

Pete glared back and wrinkled his nose to bare his teeth ever so slightly to one side of his mouth.

"I will get even with you later, my friend," he growled and walked out of the room in protest.

"Something wrong with Pete?" Ben watched as the dog turned toward the kitchen.

"I think he needs to go out for a bathroom break. It's been quite a while since he's been out. I better open the door for him." Jake followed the dog to the kitchen.

When he entered the small but well-furnished kitchen, he saw Pete with his mouth around the doorknob in a desperate attempt to turn it without success. "Can I give you a hand with that?"

"Hand, indeed. I used to have a couple of those before I assisted the first human like you. That got me exiled to the animal world. After that, even the simplest tasks could be difficult to accomplish. I guess that's all part of my eternal punishment."

Pete waited but Jake didn't open the door. "Okay, big guy, don't just stand there. Open it."

Jake turned the drool-covered doorknob, allowing Pete to walk into the garden that made up Ben's back yard.

"This is really nice. I wouldn't have expected this in the city."

The dog stretched and looked around, taking in the various vines and flowers that hung anywhere that something could hang. Pete walked over to the nicest bed of flowers and lifted his leg. Obviously, he had been holding his bladder far too long. A river of urine drenched the plants and flowed over the brick edging into the lawn before pooling at the dog's feet.

All at once, he seemed more nervous and alert. "We need to get out of here, and I mean now. Something's wrong, I can feel it." He kept his tone quiet so no one outside of the yard would hear.

"You're probably just feeling upset about taking Ben with us. You'll get over it once we get on the road."

Jake watched as Pete scratched and kicked the grass with his hind legs. "I haven't seen you do that before."

"Once in a while, the animal in me must have its way. It likes to scratch after elimination, especially if there's some grass to throw. But, uh, Jake, I was serious when I said something is wrong. The feeling is getting to be overwhelming. We need to go back inside right now and tell that fool friend of yours goodbye, or else he should grab anything he thinks he will need. We have got to get moving."

Jake was beginning to sense something oppressive in the air as well, as though something dark was closing in on them.

"Yeah, I'm feeling it now too. Come on."

"I need a minute... some privacy. Go on without me." Pete was walking in a circle in the lush grass.

Jake jogged back to the steps and into the house. He left the door open for the dog who was halfway into dropping a load on the healthy lawn.

"Ben, whatever you think you are going to need on the road, better grab it now. We need to leave here right away," Jake shouted as he ran to the front window of the home.

Cautiously, he pulled back the thick curtain and peered through the gap. Chills gripped his spine. There were more demon-possessed people standing in the yard than he could count from his vantage point, and they seemed to be honing in on the house.

Ben stepped out of his office to find out what all the shouting was about and discovered Jake peering through the small opening in the curtains.

"What is it?"

"Your whole yard is full of demon-crazed people. We need to get out of here!"

Ben stepped to the wooden door and checked the locks. He pulled a heavy metal bar from the corner and fitted one end into a metal bracket on the floor. The other end went into a similar bracket mounted on the door.

"This will hold them for a minute. Was there anyone out back?"

"No, but your yard is fenced. I couldn't see over the..."

Just then, Pete ran into the room sniffing the air. "They're right outside."

Jake stepped away from the window and waved frantically at Ben.

"Get your stuff together."

"I'm going. Make sure *you* have everything. Grab your bag and don't forget the book and the scroll. You and Pete wait at the back door, I'll be right there."

With that, he turned and bounded up the stairs. Jake ran into the office to gather his things, but Pete was a step ahead of him. He'd already put the book into the bag and was about to grab the scroll off the desk with his teeth.

"I'll get that," Jake shouted. "Is there anything else I'm forgetting?"

"Take the skull," Pete said, his voice calm, but he was panting nervously.

"For what? Are you feeling all right? Seems like an odd request."

"I'm fine, my friend. I'm thinking that skull might come in handy at some point."

Jake grabbed the fake skull and shoved it into his bag. He could hear Ben moving around in an upper room as the pounding on the door began. Quickly, it began to sound like thunder as more and more people joined in.

"Ben, what the hell? Let's go," he yelled toward the stairway.

Just as the words left his lips, he heard Ben's clunking footsteps coming down the stairs. In a moment, he came into the room from the kitchen with an assortment of swords and knives draped on his body in various places.

"Let's boogie!"

Six

The trio stepped out into the back yard, their eyes scanning all directions while they quietly made their way to the small garage. Ben unlocked the side door and carefully opened it to look inside.

"Clear," he whispered trying not to draw any attention. The crowd of possessed people were working themselves into a mass frenzy as they tried smashing in the front door of the house.

Ben patted the van like an old friend as he walked around it.

"She's old, but I had a new engine put in her. Get in." He opened the driver side door and climbed in. "Most of these babies were made with standard transmissions, but I had her rebuilt. I'm much more comfortable with the automatic in the traffic around here."

"I don't think I ever saw one of these vans before. It looks kind of cool, like a small bus or something," Jake whispered as he sat in the passenger seat while Pete climbed in the back.

"We're all going to die in this thing," Pete moaned through gritted teeth. "All these windows... They'll be trying to jump through them once we pull out of here."

"Fasten your seat belt, Jake. I had them added with the rebuild. You're gonna be glad you have it on when you see what she can do."

"Uh, what about the garage door?"

Jake could hear pounding on the outside as the demonic mob tried to beat it down. Ben turned the key and revved the engine.

"I'll get it fixed later!" he yelled over the roar of the engine and threw the van in reverse.

For a second, the tires failed to grip the concrete floor as they spun blue gray smoke into the air. Jake looked over at Ben and noticed that he had his foot on the brake pedal. Just as he opened his mouth to speak, the professor lifted his foot and the van lurched backwards into the sunlight.

CRA-SMASH! The old wooden door exploded into the faces of the group that had been trying to break into the garage. They fled side to side as Ben's customized van plowed through them. The others who had gathered out at the sidewalk were forced to jump out of the way, as the van continued into the street.

When the rear tires hit the asphalt, Ben cut the wheel and the vehicle slid sideways and continued travelling backwards about half a block before he stopped. The crowd of attackers poured out into the street and began running toward them.

Ben's first impulse was to put the van in gear and mow them down, but deep down he realized these were hapless souls, some of them neighbors. Instead of plowing through, he stepped on the gas and continued backwards until he came to a wide driveway. He whipped the wheel around and bumped up over the curb, narrowly missing a car parked in the street.

"Damn! That was close."

He took a breath while shifting into drive and then floored it again. One of the leaders of the pack had caught up with them and got himself caught between the van and its path of escape. Jake closed his eyes as the van thumped over the man.

No sooner had he opened his eyes again, than a woman took a flying leap and managed to get a foot on the running board at the base of Jake's door. The raging she-monster hung onto the side mirror with one hand while she pounded her free hand against the glass trying to break it. Jake winced as her second swing hit just right and the broken glass rained in on him. He tried to dodge the bleeding, grasping hand clutching at him.

"Open the door, Jake, now!" Pete barked from the floor of the back seat.

The woman was still dangling and trying to get a better grip on the door. The boy did as instructed, and she bounced off a wooden telephone pole and rolled to a stop on the sidewalk in their wake.

"I keep trying to tell the folks down at City Hall that those poles are too close to the street." Ben broke out in a roar of laughter. "Where are we headed?"

Jake's eyes were bugging out. He failed to find the humor in the whole mess.

"I need to stop by Maire's house and tell her we're leaving. I can't just go without saying goodbye."

"Maire's house it is then. Just tell me when to turn."

"Left here," Jake said. He grew silent as he considered how he and Pete would have gotten out of that situation alive if Ben hadn't helped them. Any doubts he'd had about bringing the man along were long forgotten.

"Jake, please tell me we are not taking the girl with us on this journey." Pete was standing with his front paws on the center console. "It's too dangerous. You realize that now, I suppose."

"Don't worry. I just want to say goodbye."

"Is Pete complaining about my driving?" Ben asked as they waited for the light to change.

"No, he's worried that Maire will be going to Georgia with us."

"Rightly so, this looks to be a dangerous mission." Ben accelerated as the light turned green. "It might be best to listen to your friend on this."

"I hear ya." Jake nodded, but he somehow he knew it wasn't going to be easy to convince Maire. Not this time.

SEVEN

"What do you mean he got away?"

Seraphine's eyes flashed with fire as she yelled her disapproval. "It was an easy enough task. Now we'll have to try to track them down wherever they are headed."

"The servant who reported it says they had some help, some middle-aged teacher who drove the getaway vehicle." Betlamel cringed waiting for some kind of pain to be rained upon him. "We will find him, you can rest assured, Mistress."

"Yes, or there *will* be hell to pay. Put the word out that the next group to fail their mission will be incinerated."

The girl clenched her fists as she stared out the window. Her anger was focused on Betlamel. He cringed as droplets of blood ran from his ears. He had expected punishment, but this was far worse than he'd anticipated.

"Take me to the Shangri-La hotel. We'll figure this out from there. I think I will enjoy owning it for a while."

"Yes, mistress. It's a very nice place," Frogoth replied. "We are headed there now."

EIGHT

At last, Jake emerged from the house, but he did not look pleased. Maire was directly behind him, and she was carrying a small suitcase. Ben and Pete watched from inside the van, which was parked next to the curb, where they had been waiting for over half an hour.

Pete began to rant, "How did I know this was going to happen? You send him in to say goodbye, and here he comes with the girl in tow." He snarled, "He needs to practice some of his vocal voodoo skills or learn to just say no."

"I agree, he shouldn't be bringing her into this..." Ben stopped mid-sentence. "Wait a minute! Did you say he should learn to say no?"

"Did I stutter? That's exactly what I said," Pete growled.

"Why am I able to hear you now? I mean I can understand what you're saying."

"Because, Professor, I'm getting bored with this 'he said, he said' business. If we're going to be working together, we need to be able to communicate." Pete's voice was calm and expressionless as if this was an everyday occurrence. "Just remember, I can shut you out at any time, funny man, so let's keep this between us. Okay? Don't tell Jake about it just yet."

Jake opened the car door for Maire. He took the suitcase from her as she climbed in and tucked it behind the bench seat.

"Hi Pete!" She smiled and ran her hand down the dog's back. Turning, she held her hand out to Ben who was checking out the pretty young woman who had just invaded his space. "You must be Ben. I'm Maire."

Ben took her hand and gave it a cordial shake. "Jake has spoken highly of you, young lady. I see now why he is so enamored with you. However, I thought he was coming to say goodbye, not to pick you up."

"Oh, he tried to say goodbye, but I wouldn't hear of it." she answered in a sing-song musical tone.

Jake opened the front passenger door and climbed in. As he slammed it shut, small geometric pieces of glass fell to the floor.

"Ben, this is Maire."

"We've met."

He could barely hide his frustration with Jake bringing the girl. He put the car into gear and pulled out into the flow of traffic.

"Now, where to? You want to go say goodbye to your boss at the store?"

Pete barked, "Jake, you know we all might die on this journey. Why did you bring her along?"

"Like I had a choice?"

"Never underestimate the power of a woman who knows what she wants," Ben interrupted.

"Oh, I see how it is," Maire cut in. "Leave the poor little girl behind. The poor little thing, she can't take care of herself." Her tone changed, taking on an air of confidence. "Look, I'm not a helpless whiner, you know. I can probably kick all your asses."

"Sure, Joan of Arc, go ahead and lead the charge." Pete rolled his eyes. "I can't take much more of this."

"No, she's right. Maire's been practicing martial arts for a few years now. I guess you didn't know she's an accomplished fighter with a black belt," Jake defended her. "Actually, she'll be a great asset for us to have along, now that I think about it."

"Yeah, and a boat anchor is a great asset to have on a sailboat," Pete cracked.

Ben agreed, "Yeah, and don't forget the albatross and the ancient mariner."

Jake looked at Ben and back at Pete, then again at Ben. "Pull over a minute, there, at that plaza." He pointed the way. Ben slowed and pulled into the parking lot.

As he rolled to a stop, Jake opened the door and climbed out. "Can I have a word with you, Ben?" He walked away from the van and Ben followed.

"What now?" Maire complained. "Is it gonna be a boys club all the way to Atlanta?"

"Doesn't sound too bad to me," Pete growled, as Maire sat back with her arms folded.

A few yards away, Jake was animated, waving his arms as he talked to Ben. "You can understand Pete now? How did that happen?"

"I don't know," he shrugged. "You were in the house with Maire, and we were waiting, just sitting there for like half an hour. All of a sudden, I could understand him. He said he was 'letting me' understand him. Not sure what that means, but he said he can stop any time he wants."

"Damn. After all this time... and making me translate? I wonder if he is going to let Maire in on this too?"

"Who knows? He told me not to tell you about it." He stuck his hands in his pockets. "Honestly, I'd rather not have to ask you to translate all the time, if you don't mind, and Maire's not going to appreciate being shut out. You might as well ask Pete to let her in."

"He has a mind of his own, as you may have learned by now. He might be intent on torturing her a bit longer."

Jake turned and started to walk back toward the van. He stopped for a moment to add, "If I were to be honest, I'm glad she's going with us. Of course, I am afraid for her safety. With what we've seen so far, we might all end up dead. I hate to think of what could happen."

"Well, my friend, let's not think about it that way. Stay focused on the mission." Ben used his hands in a gesture that indicated tunnel vision. "Before we head out, is there anything else you need to take with us? Perhaps something from the bank you left the last time you were there?"

"Yes, there are a couple of things: First, I need to get everything from the safe deposit box. We may not come back this way again for some time, and I don't want to leave anything behind that we might need. Second, didn't you mention that you knew someone who could set Pete up with the service dog certification?"

"I don't recall such a conversation."

"No, wait, it was the vet." Jake pulled a crumpled piece of paper from his pocket and handed it to Ben. "Do you know where this is?"

"Sure, we can stop there on our way to the bank." He grabbed the door handle as he shouted over the van to Jake, who was headed to the passenger side. "The bad guys know where we are now. We'd better get out of town as soon as possible."

"Bad *guys*. Don't forget there could be women and children, too. I don't think this kind of evil follows any rules," Jake responded. He opened the passenger door and climbed into the seat.

"You are correct if you are speaking of my kind, Jake. They will kill us by any means possible, and they take no prisoners. All they want is the skin off your back," Pete whined.

Ben wasn't sure he was better off now that he could understand what was just said.

"Is he always the voice of gloom and doom?"

"No, Teacher-man, only when it's necessary to illustrate the folly of fools. You want humor? A dog walks into a 15th century pub..." Pete howled, as Maire glared at the three of them.

NINE

Ben and Pete sat in the van while Jake and Maire went into the bank to retrieve the remaining contents from the safe deposit box. Pete was sporting his brand new service dog vest and guide harness. He seemed quite pleased with the way he looked in it.

"I think this red vest complements my glossy black fur rather well, don't you?"

"I have to admit, it is a good color on you," Ben said without looking at the dog. His gaze was riveted on the bank's exit doors. He was anxious to get Jake and Maire back in the van and get on the road. "I wish they would hurry up," he muttered nervously. "We're too exposed sitting here like this."

Inside, Jake was signing the sheet on the clipboard before being escorted into the vault of deposit boxes. The bank employee unlocked Jake's box and set it on the table.

"If you need anything else, let me know. I will be just outside."

"Could you get my girlfriend a glass of water? I'd appreciate it."

Turning, he excused himself. "Certainly, Mr. Rune."

Maire was sitting in the waiting area when she saw the man exit the vault. He seemed in a hurry as he scooted into a back room. She turned to look at all of the people standing in line at the teller windows and missed seeing the man coming out of the room again. He slipped back into the vault, stepping unnoticed through the arched door, and pulling a length of cord from his pocket.

Jake was zipping up the bag when the man drew up behind him and wrapped the ends of the cord tightly around each hand, lurching forward to slip it around Jake's neck and pull it tight. The boy was caught completely off guard and stumbled backward as the cord began to cut into his throat.

The man lost his balance as Jake fell backwards into him and slammed into the wall of deposit boxes. The element of surprise gave Jake the opportunity he needed to ease the tension of the cord. With his left foot, he braced himself as he brought up his right foot. He aimed for the side of the man's kneecap and put his full force into a kick that snapped the man's leg and sent the two of them sprawling to the floor.

The attacker should have been screaming in pain, but there was no reaction. He certainly was not letting up on the cord, and Jake started to cough and choke from the pressure. He was lying on the floor in front of the would-be killer with nothing there to grasp that he might use to regain his footing.

Maire heard the scuffle coming from the vault. Since Jake was there merely to empty a box, she became curious and went to the vault door to investigate. She stifled a scream as she saw Jake's face turning purple and the man behind him attempting to choke the life from him. Though her heart fluttered with more than a twinge of panic, she knew exactly what she had to do.

With three bounding steps forward, she landed a downward stomp on the man's arm at the elbow, coming down as hard as she could. She could see by the awkward angle that – "SNAP" – it was sure to break. The man did not scream as she expected, but he did lose his grip on the cord.

Jake did not hesitate to take advantage of the moment. He rolled over and brought the palm of his hand up slapping the broken killer on the forehead. Maire jumped back, stunned at the hideous demon that split away from the head of the man. More horrible than either that had possessed her mom and sister, the beast snapped furiously at Jake with its foul jaws as he grabbed it by the head and pulled the rest of it from the man's body.

Instantly, his attacker fell limp against the wall of boxes as the demon came loose. Jake pushed himself from the floor with one hand and held the thrasher in the other. Once he got to his feet, he stomped on it with his left foot to hold it down.

Outside the vault, it was business as usual. No one seemed aware as Jake recited the words to dispel the evil just steps away in the privacy of the vault. Even the terrible howling of the demon as it burned to ash was inaudible to the crowd. Not one person waiting in any of the lines showed any indication of concern.

"Grab the bag and walk casually out to the van. I'm right behind you," Jake instructed Maire as he took hold of the man by the shirt and pulled him as far away from the vault door as possible.

"What about him?" she hesitated.

"Don't worry, I'll handle it. Please, go quickly!"

Maire turned and strolled through the building as casually as she could manage under the circumstances. She walked straight out the front door without looking back.

Meanwhile, Jake placed the box back in its slot and locked it. He put the keys into the unconscious man's hand before exiting the vault, closing the metal bar door behind him. As he took the sign-in sheet from the clipboard on the desk, he wasn't sure if he could successfully erase his presence. He figured it was worth a try.

Taking a deep breath, he walked into the middle of the room. With a deep and hypnotically forceful voice, he loudly announced, "Fire! Everyone out!"

Everyone turned and ran for the doors, as he walked quickly toward them. Merging into the crowd, he was pushed along by the wave of panicked women and men. Once outside, he strolled casually to the van and climbed in.

"Maire was just telling us about the guy who attacked you. What happened?" Ben had already started the van and was putting it in gear as he spoke.

Jake looked over his shoulder as they pulled away. "Someone yelled that the bank was on fire." He smiled and rubbed his throat, which had already healed from the attempt on his life.

"Would that someone be sitting right in front of me?" Maire leaned forward and rubbed his shoulders over the back of the seat.

"Let's just say... a little voice in their heads suggested it." Jake laughed and put his hands on hers.

"Now the boy can manipulate whole groups of people? That hasn't been done by any of the others that came before him," Pete growled.

Ben turned the corner. *I can't wait to see what else he can do*, he thought and headed for the freeway on-ramp.

TEN

About 1 a.m., the group was about ten miles north of Richmond, Virginia, when the engine on the van began to sputter.

"Oh, not now, Shirley. Not here!" Ben wailed as he headed for the side of the highway.

Jake and Maire were asleep in the back seat and Pete had been riding shotgun.

"Who is Shirley? No one here goes by that name."

"Oh yes sir, buddy, this old girl has been called Shirley since I bought her." Ben patted the dashboard. "She's about to die on us, I'm afraid."

Pete let the buddy comment pass. "I didn't know that machines could die. Is it because you ran her through the door of her stable? That kind of impact would injure most... animals."

Ben laughed out loud. "She's not alive, Pete, not like any kind of animal at least. But she is about to shut down on me, and that's just as bad as dying where a machine is concerned."

As the old van made its final gasp, the professor stepped on the brake and came to a stop well off the pavement.

"Jake, wake up." He turned to see the two young adults in the back curled around each other and lying halfway down on the seat. "Jake!" he said louder causing him to wake.

"What? What's wrong? Why are we stopping here?"

"The engine just died. I have no idea what's wrong with it." About then, he realized there was smoke rising from the rear engine compartment.

"Everybody out, quick! Grab your things, this thing's about to burst into flames!"

"I thought you said you had the engine replaced."

Jake was still half asleep and helping Maire out the side door when a huge eighteen-wheeler roared past.

"The bags, Jake." Maire reached back in and handed him both of their bags. "Come on Pete, watch out for the cars."

"Don't mess with the service dog vest," Pete growled as he jumped out into the wet grass.

Ben scrambled around to the passenger side. One of the samurai swords was dragging on the ground as he carried the assortment of weapons. Dumping the load at Jakes feet, he hurried to the back of the van.

As he opened the door to the engine compartment, the sudden burst of fresh air caused the engine to burst into flames. A line of traffic zoomed by drowning out Ben's stream of profanities.

Jake yelled, "Get back from the gas tank!"

No sooner did the words escape his lips than the gas tank exploded. Immediately, the van was engulfed in a roaring fire. Ben staggered back, shaking his head and muttering something unintelligible before dropping to his knees. Tears streamed down the man's face.

"Ben, don't worry, man. We'll get you another one." Jake put his hand on the man's shoulder. "We'll find one just like her."

"It will never be like Shirley, a lot of memories in that old girl."

"It sounds so strange, all this talk about a machine as though it were a person. I've not seen such attachment before." Pete took a more sympathetic tone and added, "I'm sorry for your loss, Ben. She was a great warrior."

He sat down next to Ben and waited as the man dealt with his grief. Right about then, a woman in a large black SUV slowed, flipped on her turn signal and pulled over a short distance down the road. The backup lights came on as she put the truck in reverse and maneuvered closer to them.

"Oh my goodness, are y'all okay? Is anybody hurt?" She was an older woman with graying hair and a bulky sweater draped over her shoulders.

Ben was trying to compose himself and stood wiping the tears from his face and brushing himself off. Maire looked over at Jake before replying, "I think we're fine. Could you give us a ride to the nearest motel?"

"Well certainly, my dear. Uh, does the dog bite?" She was looking over the girl's shoulder at Pete who was still at Ben's side and busy scratching his ear, his vest flailing wildly in the dim light.

"Oh no, he's a service dog, very well trained," she answered with a subtle wink at Jake.

"Well, in that case, gather your things and load 'em up. We'll get you to a warm, safe place."

The woman walked back to the SUV and opened the tailgate. As she turned to wait for them, she noticed Ben gathering the weapons from the ground. Maire saw the shocked expression on her face and did not want to lose the opportunity to get a ride.

"We're, uh, actors," she offered with a smile, "on our way to Atlanta for the opening of our new show." She wasn't sure about the theatres in Atlanta but she was hoping she could fake her way through this.

"Oh! Are you going to be at the Fox Theater? What's the name of the play?"

"Camelot. It's why we have the swords." Ben set them in the back of the truck and then helped Jake with the bags.

"Oh, I do love that show. I saw it once in New York, on Broadway so many years ago. Who's playing King Arthur this season, anyone I know?"

"Is this woman for real? She actually believes you are actors?" Pete growled softly.

"Brad Pitt!" Maire blurted.

"So handsome, that man is. Almost too pretty to play the king." She shut the tailgate. "Let's hurry then, you must be tired."

As the group piled into the SUV, Ben looked back one last time at his beloved Shirley before settling into the front passenger seat. His heart was heavy. He figured he would never see his old van again.

"I'm really gonna miss it," he sighed getting misty-eyed again.

The woman switched on her turn signal and pulled out onto the highway. Leaning over to Ben, she patted him on the knee and whispered, "I know just how you feel. I lost my virginity in one of those. Of course, that was a long time ago." She laughed, and Ben couldn't help but laugh with her through his tears.

ELEVEN

Jake and Maire were asleep, each in their own Queen-sized bed, when Pete howled at them, "Rise and shine, people. We're burning daylight!"

Jake heeded the wake up call while Maire covered her ears to muffle the howls. "Can't you do something about that animal?" she whined.

"Pete, come on, man. We're awake already."

"You certainly do sleep late for someone on a mission of such importance. We need to keep moving. What's the plan?" The dog sat waiting impatiently for an answer.

"Well, seeing as how the van has burned up, we need to get a new car or something…" He was interrupted by heavy pounding on the door.

"Everything okay in there? Jake? Pete?"

Jake walked to the door, looked through the peephole and opened it. Ben stood in the hall in his red boxer shorts. He didn't seem to realize it until Jake broke out in a broad grin.

"Nice boxers, Ben. I didn't know they made them in that shade of red. Kinda matches your face right about now." He laughed.

Embarrassed, Ben headed back to his room. "Very funny, wise guy. Get ready, we need to be out of here in less than an hour." The last words faded off before he slammed the door shut behind him.

"What's wrong with him?" Maire asked as she exited the bathroom.

"I think he heard Pete howling and thought something was wrong. He wants to leave soon. You should get a shower right away if you're going to get one."

Jake closed the door and checked beside the dresser where he had stowed his bag.

"I need to get some new clothes, these are pretty nasty. We'll have to stop by the bank and check my balance. We're going to need a new vehicle so we can get to Atlanta."

"You don't have to go to the bank, silly. Just call the number on the back of your card. Give it to me, I'll call for you." Maire held out her hand.

Pete rolled his eyes at the two of them, "Anything she says, Jake? Let me out so I can go relieve myself."

Maire glared at the growling dog.

"Give us a minute, would ya?" Jake answered. "I need to find out what kind of cash I have to work with before we spend it all on a new car."

The dog walked over to the window and pulled back the curtain with his teeth. He jumped up on the chair situated nearby so he could look outside at the sunny day.

"No problem, my friend, I'll just hold it," he whined sarcastically.

Jake pulled the bankcard from his wallet and handed it to Maire. She took a seat on the bed next to the phone, checked the back of the card and dialed. A moment later, "It's asking for your pin number. Punch it in for me."

Jake entered the pin number he had memorized and waited. Maire held the phone up to her ear and listened. She turned a whiter shade of pale as she slowly hung up the phone. Silent, she sat staring at the bed across from her.

"Well, are you gonna tell me or…"

Suddenly, she came out of her trance, jumping from the bed and hopping up and down.

"Jake… we're, I mean *you're* rich!" she squeaked, trying to catch her breath.

"How much did it say?"

Maire hopped over to him and got right up in his face. "Five million, one hundred and twenty six thousand… and something."

She let out a squeal and began hopping around again before stopping in front of him again. "Jake, oh my gosh! My ears shut down before I got the rest."

Jake couldn't speak. He put his hands on his stomach and sat down on the foot of the bed.

"I don't… understand… We always lived like everyone else, a small apartment with just enough to live on, while there was all of this money." He gazed down at the floor deep in thought.

Maire didn't know how to respond to his sudden change in mood. She couldn't tell if he was happy or sad. She offered what she could.

"I've heard of that before, a family member passes away after years of living a humble existence, and then her relatives discover that all along she had millions." She paused.

Getting no reaction, she went on, "Your grandmother knew you had important things to do. I'm guessing she sacrificed everything to make sure you could accomplish them."

"But she wasn't even really my grandmother!" Jake looked at Maire and she could see his tears. "She didn't have to do this for me."

"Maybe it wasn't her choice to make. What if someone gave her the money and instructed her to save it for you. Maybe that was *her* mission. I mean, it's possible, you know?"

"Yeah, I know. I guess it isn't going to help to stop and question any of it now. Let's just get ready to go.

You can have the shower first." He wanted to talk to Ben anyway. "I'll be back in a minute."

"Hey, outside?" Pete jumped from the chair and nudged him.

"Yeah, buddy, let's go." He opened the door and the dog followed him out into the hall and the elevator.

"Jake, I guess you found out you have quite a bit of money? The girl seems so happy about it. Money usually makes them... more agreeable." Pete sneered.

"Yeah. We can discuss it later. Right now, I need some quiet so I can think."

"Sure, the dog should know its place, speak only when it's spoken to and all that. Let me know when you need saving again, okay? I'll be right here by your side until then, all quiet and doglike." Pete let his head droop.

"Oh come on. Let's go take care of your, um, need." Jake gave Pete a crooked smile and added, "Crazy dog!" He rubbed Pete's head to piss him off.

TWELVE

"What kind of car are we looking for Jake?"

Maire was reading the window tag of a red convertible sports car and dreaming of her hair blowing in the wind on a warm and sunny day, just her and Jake, out in the country, with no other cars on the road. *How awesome would that be,* she thought.

Jake snapped her back into the moment. "We need something powerful and durable after what happened yesterday."

He walked toward the sport utility vehicles and trucks hoping she would follow. Pete was trotting beside him and checking out all of the different types of trucks from his point of view.

"I liked the days when people rode horses. They smelled bad, but you could have some fun with them when they weren't working."

"Now what would we do with horses? We wouldn't be able to get all of our stuff on a few horses. We'd need a wagon, and it would take forever to get where we need to go."

Jake was checking out the rack on the front of a truck and considering whether they could use it to crash through a wall if it became necessary.

"I know, you have all your devices, and we do have to travel far, but still..."

"Whatever we get will need to have air conditioning," Jake interrupted.

"Yeah, I just love these cold, lifeless pieces of metal. Which one will you choose? Will you give a name to yours too?"

The dog lifted his leg and urinated on the wheel of the truck Jake was scrutinizing.

"Hey guys, wait up," Ben called from across the lot. He caught up to them after paying the cab driver. "That was a seventy-five dollar cab ride. I think it's cheaper in New York City than it is around here."

He walked up to where they stood looking at a shiny black four-wheeler and nodded. "That one looks like it means business."

With a sturdy rack attached to the front grill, it looked as though it could plow through just about anything. Besides that, it had an integrated winch. All of the windows were tinted a dark color and there was a lack of chrome that ensured it would not stand out in the dark of night; exactly the stealth they might require in their future endeavors. Jake was trying the locked door when a salesman slinked up behind them.

"Anybody helping y'all?" he inquired in a slimy southern drawl. "Name's Tom."

He shoved a wrinkled business card into Ben's hand. "That's a beauty for sure, the only one like it I ever seen on the lot. We call it, *The Beast*. Lemme get some keys for ya, and we'll take her for a ride."

He hesitated a moment as though expecting some push back before spinning on his heel and heading for the sales office to retrieve the keys.

"He doesn't any waste time," observed Maire as she cupped her hands around her eyes to try and see through the tinted window. "I can't see anything at all in there."

Ben agreed. It was difficult to see anything through the windows.

"That's what we need, complete anonymity. The less people can see inside, the better for us. Tell you what, Jake, if this thing drives as good as it looks, we should consider it."

"My thought exactly. What do you say, Pete?"

"It's black. I'm black. I like black."

Jake was giving him a look.

"What?" Pete cocked his head. "If it's all black inside, I think you should take it."

Right about then a chirping sound came from the doors as the salesman unlocked them from across the lot. There was a cigarette dangling from his mouth and he tossed it just before he came up to the group gathered around the truck.

"Everybody in, except whoever is going to stay here with the dog."

Pete growled at the man and bared his teeth. "I'm not staying here. Tell him about my vest."

Jake was still glaring.

"Okay. I'm sorry. The truck is perfect," Pete quickly made amends.

"Uh, I need to take the dog with us," Jake told the salesman. "He's my service dog."

Ben opened the front passenger door and got in, saying, "It's against federal law to deny access to a service dog. Should we call 911 to have this verified for you?"

The salesman was speechless and stood frowning at the dog. Finally, he noticed the service dog label on the vest.

"Well... I was wondering why he was wearing a jacket on a warm day like this. Okay then, everybody in, but I'll have to drive it off the lot. After we get around the corner, you can take over."

He opened the door on the driver's side and climbed in. "Which one of you are lookin' to take *The Beast* home today?"

Maire was feeling spunky and answered him straight away, "It's the dog's car. Are you going to give us a hard time about him test driving it too?"

The salesman nearly swerved into a pole as he steered the vehicle out of the lot. "Missy, I hope you're joking, because vest or no vest, that dog is not going to be driving with me today." His voice cracked as he squeaked his ultimatum.

"I'll be driving it," Ben broke in to keep the salesman from crashing. "Let's just get through this, Tom. I think you are going to have some paperwork to fill out when we get back."

The man perked up when he heard this.

"Here we are. I could tell this one was made just for y'all when I saw you looking at her."

He parked the car and got out to trade sides with Ben.

THIRTEEN

"What in hell's name are those people doing?"

Seraphine threw the tea she had been sipping across the room. "How are we supposed to peel the skin from that fool's back when they keep moving around?"

She stood up from her luxuriously cushioned chair and walked over to the double doors leading out to the patio that was part of her penthouse suite. Throwing them open with enough force to rattle the glass, she stepped out into the dark moonless night. In the distance, the light from the Eiffel Tower shot into the overcast sky casting an eerie glow over the city.

Frogoth approached her cautiously from behind. "Mistress, do you need me to call our people in this city, Richmond, and have them find out what they are doing?"

She spun around and glared at him, "And what good would that do? By the time that we could get our servants mobilized, the little band of rodents may have moved on to some other location. We need a better way to track them."

Betlamel stood off to one side of the doors inside the room and took the question as his cue to step from the shadows and share his limited knowledge of such things.

"Begging your forgiveness, Mistress, I believe the solution to this problem is in the air." He pointed at the ceiling as he spoke.

"What are you saying, you moron? You think we can see them from the sky? Are you an idiot? What kind of magic would we need for that?"

He was beginning to think he should have kept his mouth shut. "Not magic. You must ask the crows for their help. They have been our eyes and ears in the past."

When it seemed she wished to hear more, he continued, "You must call the crows from the rooftops and tell them to spread the word."

"By the time our crows fly to America and talk to some crows over there, who knows where they will be. No, that is much too slow."

"But mistress, they have their own way to communicate, and it is faster than you might think. I don't know how it works, but it is very efficient."

Betlamel glanced over at Frogoth and back to Seraphine, keeping his gaze lowered. "Call the crows and they will come to you from out of the blackness of night."

She wasn't sure that she believed his story. She turned and raised her hands.

"Crows of the night, in darkness, in flight, come do my bidding to guide in our fight." She began to laugh. "That's it? You dimwit, I should throw you over the rail for your foolishness!"

She raised her hand toward her cowering servant when out of the dark skies came the sound of fluttering wings. A murder of crows began to land all around her. As she turned to get a look at them, they settled on the rail behind her, on the furniture, and on the ledge above the open doors. One very large fellow landed directly on the ground at her feet and looked up at her with black lifeless eyes.

"Why did you call us from our sleep?" he demanded.

"You speak? I must be dreaming."

She rubbed her eyes as the voice inside her assured, *"We are not asleep. Tell the creature what we need."*

"Indeed, we speak, but only to those who can hear. Pray tell, why did you summon us? Reveal your purpose, or perhaps we should return to the rooftops?"

"Do not speak to me as my equal, bird, or you will be but a stain of blood and feathers on my floor. I need you to call to your kind across the ocean. We must locate someone there and quickly."

The crow ruffled its feathers and began to caw, jeering, "So you threaten me and *then* ask for my help? Obviously you are not familiar with..." The bird began to choke.

Seraphine held her fist tightly closed before her. "You will do as I say, or you all will be as rain. I will shower the people walking below with your blood as you fall dead from this balcony."

She slowly released her grip on the bird, and it bowed low asking in a more reverent tone, "Over which ocean would you have us cross, my queen?"

"The Atlantic, to Virginia, the city of Richmond, to be exact. However, the ones we seek are on the move. We will need to have constant vigil."

The crow had maintained its more submissive stance allowing Seraphine to relax. She made an attempt at humor. "You must follow them straight to their destination as the crow flies."

"As the crow flies? Indeed. And how will my friends know who it is they seek?"

"They will look for the small band of humans and the black dog."

She waved her hand over the marble floor. The lines in the marble shifted to form the image of Jake as well as the others.

"When you find their resting place, you will relay the message to my minions here." She motioned to the thugs who stood silently by. "Can you do this?"

"Yes, we will find them and will inform you immediately thereafter. Is there anything else I may do for you on this night?" The crow shifted its weight as it raised its wings and prepared to fly.

"Yes, one more thing." She bent down to speak directly into the face of the bird.

"Fail me, and your kind will never again be found in the skies of Paris. Ever. Again."

FOURTEEN

The group sat in a line of cars waiting to go through the gate at Stone Mountain Park with Ben behind the wheel. Jake was asleep in the back seat with Maire tucked under his arm. Pete sat in the front content to watch the passing pine trees that lined most roads in the area.

The park ranger at the gate waved at them to move forward, and Ben handed him the entry fee to get into the park. Pete was getting nervous. He didn't like crowds. There could people around who were possessed like the ones that had attacked them at Ben's house and such individuals could make their move before he had a chance to detect who or where they were.

"It will be easier to sense any danger once we reach our destination. Walk me around a bit before Jake gets out so I can get a feel for the people." Pete turned toward the back seat. "Judging from the sounds coming from back there last night, these two might like a moment alone."

Jake was awake now. "I'm fine with that. While you two go exploring, I'll check the book again to see whether any additional information is available before we search for the scroll." Unzipping his bag, he checked to make sure that the book was still there.

"Okay then, here we are." Ben pulled the beast of a vehicle into a parking space. "I'm going to leave the engine running and the air conditioner on, otherwise you two will quickly become uncomfortable in this heat. Lock the doors when we get out."

Once the doors were locked, Jake pulled the book from the bag and opened it. Maire watched as he slid the knife out of its pocket inside the cover.

"The pages are blank, Jake. How can you read a book with blank pages?"

"Yeah, I know. Strange huh? Watch this." With the book resting on his lap, Jake made a deep cut in the palm of his hand.

"Ooooh, what are you doing? I think I'm going to be sick." Maire looked away as he allowed the blood to drip from his hand to the center of the page.

"That's it. Look, my hand has already healed." He wiped the excess on the page. "Maire, look."

"No, I don't want to see."

"The blood is gone. The book soaks it up. Look."

Jake held up the book, pushing it into her line of peripheral vision. She turned her head slightly and squinted as if to reduce her exposure to whatever she expected to see.

"Hey, how did the writing get there?"

"From what we've figured out so far, the book absorbs the blood and uses it to write the words. I need to hurry now and see what it says before it wears off."

He pulled the book back and scanned the pages, turning them slowly. "What do you think this means?"

Jake read from the book…

Beware of the dark shadowy eyes in the sky. They seek to bring about your destruction. Climb the mountain from behind in the dark of night and extract the scroll you seek. Complete the task well before dawn to avoid those who seek to peel the scroll from your back.

"The dark shadowy eyes in the sky? What could that be?"

Jake paged back through the book looking for a hint, some clue to the meaning behind the words, but there was nothing.

Only one map had been revealed in the final pages and the glowing yellow dot confirmed that they had reached their destination. When Jake looked out the window toward the mountain, he thought he could actually see the light shining through the trees. He imagined it was coming from the face of the mountain and might show the location of the scroll if he had a clear view of the carving.

After a short walk around, Ben returned with Pete. Maire reached forward to press the unlock button and Ben opened the door.

"What did you see out there?" Jake asked.

"Pete says it's all clear, but I have a strange feeling about the whole thing. There's a large open lawn in front of the mountain. You probably need to see it for yourselves."

Ben did not move to get into the truck, and Pete stood waiting for Jake to get out.

"They have a ski lift here," Ben added, "but I don't think we should search for the scroll while the lift is running and the park is open. It would surely attract too much attention."

"Okay then, let's go have a look."

Ben leaned into the truck and retrieved the keys, and Jake stepped out of the vehicle carrying his bag. Maire quickly followed as they all headed toward the mountain.

**

"Holy crap! How high up is that?" Jake shielded his eyes with his hand as he took in the scene. It was hard to believe how someone could have carved the soldiers and their mounts on the face of the mountain. "We've got to get into the nose of one of those horse's. How are we going to accomplish that?"

He decided not to mention that he was able to visualize the exact location of the scroll. He was sure he could see a glow emanating from inside of the horse's nostril.

"My guess is it's about three hundred feet up from the ground. Climbing down from the top... maybe two hundred. I'm thinking that the scroll is hidden in the nose of first horse," Ben replied. "How the heck did they get the scroll up there?"

"Could be that one of the workers put it there when they were carving it," Maire suggested.

While the others had been scoping out the mountain, she had gone to the information building and was now holding a brochure in her hands.

"The carving is four hundred feet above the ground. It says here that it was completed in 1972. That's probably when the scroll was left there." She looked up at the massive stone wall. "We are going to have to rappel down from the top."

"No, not *we*. I'm going to do it. I've done it before... about a hundred feet or so... well, there were other people there to help..." Jake wiped his brow. "Look, there's no other way to do it that I can see."

"So after you get the scroll, then what? Are you going to climb back up?" Pete was sitting on the grass, sniffing and watching for any threat from the crowd of people.

"No, I think it will be better to rappel the rest of the way down. Only thing is, how are we going to get up there carrying that much rope? We can't do it in daylight, and the lift doesn't run at night."

Jake held his hand out to Maire and motioned her to let him look at the brochure. In a moment, he confirmed, "The skylift closes at 5 p.m. However, it says there is a trail about a mile long leading to the top. We'll have to hike up there. Uh, it's about a seven hundred foot incline from the start of the trail."

"Seven hundred foot elevation? I knew I should have gotten that gym membership last year. So we're going to have to hike straight up now, nice." Ben turned pale at the thought of it. "We'd better do this tonight, Jake. We can't stay around here for long, or any one place for that matter. We should leave and get whatever we're going to need for this."

"We need rope, lots of climbing rope, and we don't have much time."

Jake turned and started walking back to the truck with everyone falling in behind him. Though he believed he could handle the rappelling, he had butterflies in his stomach as he imagined actually doing it.

FIFTEEN

About two hours before midnight, the black truck rolled toward the park gate with its headlights off. Ahead, Jake could see the lights of the guard shacks. Two guards were outside engrossed in conversation.

As the truck rolled to a stop, Jake asked, "Now what? We need to get past those guards to get to the trail."

"We'll need to do more than that." Ben sounded nervous. "We've got to park this truck in one of the empty parking lots, and get the four of us to the trail without attracting any attention."

"You'll have to use the voice, Jake. If you do, we can get the guards to help us." Pete sounded sure.

"Look, if this dog is going to be carrying on conversations with the three of you all the time, someone should help me understand what he's saying. I am getting tired of being left out, and I'm not stepping out of this vehicle until something is done about it." Maire felt confident that she was about to get what she wanted since it was the opportune moment to ask.

"Women. Jake, correct me if I'm wrong, but didn't I warn you about bringing her along?" Pete growled.

"You're wrong. Let her hear you. It might be important when we get up there and I'm dangling over the edge, don't you think?" He glared at the dog waiting for his compliance. "Do I have to do something to convince you?"

"Oh all right," he sighed. "Are you happy now, girl? Can you hear the words that are coming out of my mouth?" He spoke deliberately slow.

"Does he always sound like that?" she asked Jake. "How annoying. I would hate to have to listen to him talk like that all of the time."

Jake shook his head and put the truck into gear, pulling up to the guards.

"The park closed at five today," the first guard announced as Jake rolled down his window.

The second guard added, "You can go over there to turn around. Follow that road back to the highway." He pointed in the direction of the exit.

"Over that way?" Jake asked in his normal voice before opening the door and stepping out of the truck. Suddenly, his voice changed growing deeper and thicker, swirling into the space between him and the guards. "We need your help with something in the park."

The guards' eyes grew wide and they nodded as Jake spoke to them. Inside the truck, Maire watched in wonder as he gave them their instructions. It was the first time she had witnessed his hypnotic power and a chill ran through her.

Jake wasn't the same guy she knew just a week ago. The boy who worked at the grocery store, the boy she had been dating had been transformed. The Jake that was climbing back into the truck was more confident, more forceful, and almost creepy in a way she wasn't sure she could fully grasp, let alone explain.

The two guards got into their truck, and the one in the driver seat rolled down his window and motioned them to follow as they drove through the gate arm. The yellow and red barrier bent slightly then snapped off, falling to the ground. Jake ran it over as the guards led the way.

Unseen, three black crows circled in the dark sky above them. One broke away and flew toward the highway. A short distance from the scene, it began to caw loudly, broadcasting the alert. Soon, a hundred others repeated the message.

SIXTEEN

The cloudy sky over Paris reflected the lights of the city making it appear bright outside at four in the morning. Seraphine lounged on the penthouse patio and inspected her fingernails intently. She had just discovered that she could make them grow at will, and better than that, change their color to match anything in nature. Currently, each nail was a different color allowing her the luxury of deciding which she liked the best.

The flutter of wings did not surprise her. She had sensed the birds approaching long before she heard them. The large crow landed on the table in front of her as she blew on her fingertips to color all of her nails a deep shade of red.

"I am hoping you have some good news for me, otherwise I am about to turn you inside out."

The bird bowed low. "Indeed I do, mistress. We have found your prey. They are in a place called Stone Mountain..."

"Don't bother me with details. Tell my minions to mobilize the horde and give them the specific location. Then leave before I decide to have some fun with you and your brethren here."

The crow looked around nervously for the two large beasts that served this wretched woman. It spread its wings and flew through the open doorway to where the thugs had fallen asleep in a couple of large chairs. Cawing loudly to wake them, the bird relayed its information and waited until they made some calls to deploy their hordes before turning to leave. There could be no errors or it would go badly for him and his kind.

"I am hoping that we do not have to meet again," the bird said in disgust before turning to fly off into the night.

Seraphine watched as the birds departed, then rose from her chair and strolled into the room.

"Have you given the order?"

"Yes, mistress. We have hundreds in that area, and all are being mobilized as we speak." Betlamel stood facing his mistress and looked as though he had something else to say.

"What is it?" She knew there was something more and hated having to ask.

"What if they fail again? Maybe we should go there ourselves." His voice trailed off at the end. He knew he should have kept his thoughts to himself and he waited for his punishment.

The young woman walked over to him, looked up at his hulking frame, and placed her pale hand on his arm. "Perhaps you are right, maybe we should go there and handle it ourselves. However, you dare to imply that I had not already thought of this?"

She curled her fingers across his bulky forearm digging her nails in deep. Betlamel howled in pain, yet he knew better than to pull his arm away when he was being punished. A blackish fluid seeped from beneath her nails as she willed them to grow deep into the bone. His pain became so intense that he dropped to his knees.

"I'm sorry, Mistress, I didn't mean to...."

"Of course, you didn't." With that, she retracted her nails and released his arm.

"Now, on your feet and back in your chair. I'm thinking we may need to go to America soon. You should be rested in case you are required to fly my jet."

Frogoth had observed the entire scene and couldn't help but ask, "You have a jet, mistress?"

Seraphine turned and glared at him. Flames shot out from her eyes in a burning stare.

"Fools, the two of you! I have anything and anyone I desire. Display your insolence again and I will be forced to replace the both of you."

SEVENTEEN

Jake, Maire, and Ben wore headbands with bright LED lights as they worked their way up the trail that led to the top of the mountain. Pete and the two park rangers followed behind them with only the moon to light their trail.

It was the dog's job to make sure the men kept up with the others and that they were kept in a state of suggestive control. He had never held anyone in that condition for so long a period before and he wasn't sure if he could maintain it for the duration of the mission. He was almost certain that Jake was strong enough to do it, but soon he would be dangling from a rope several hundred feet above the ground. It would definitely be a challenge for the dog if they snapped out of the trance while the boy was occupied.

"Holy crap! I'm starting to wonder if I can do this," Ben wheezed. "I hope the next section of trail does not head straight up the mountain."

"The brochure said it would have a handrail," Maire called back over her shoulder.

"Handrail or not, I don't think I'm gonna make it."

Jake turned around and walked back to Ben. "I can help if you want. I'll just say a few words so it won't seem so challenging."

"You think that would work? If so... aw, hell, just do it."

Ben closed his eyes and scrunched up his face as if he expected Jake to throw fairy dust in his eyes. Instead, the words swirled from the young man's lips thick and sweet as honey.

"You are as strong as a horse. You could carry us all to the top if we asked you. You are not tired, continue walking."

The change that overcame Ben was rapid and startling. He straightened, smiled and he was no longer short of breath. His stride became longer and stronger. Suddenly, the two youngsters had to scramble to keep up.

"Ben, are you sure you're okay?" Maire called ahead.

The man stopped and laughed, "Hell, I feel great. Want me to carry you?"

Maire looked over at Jake and he shrugged his shoulders. "That seems to work pretty well."

The dog and his two assigned charges had almost caught up to them.

Jake called to him, "How are your pack mules doing, Pete?"

"Pack mules indeed," Pete snorted. "At least the others like you never made me climb a mountain. There should be some limits to how much torture a dog has to endure in order to keep you safe."

He turned and glared at Jake as he passed by. "Well, I guess the others really didn't get this far so that would make the difference."

"Wait a minute... stop!" Jake pushed ahead while the dog waited for him to catch up. "Did you say the others didn't get this far? They were supposed to come here for the scroll?"

"No, no, that's not what I meant. The others did not live as long as you after the..." He turned and trailed off as he muttered under his breath, "Uh oh."

"Stop walking, dog." Jake moved up next to him.

"What do you mean they didn't live long? After what, the Awareness?" He stood above Pete with his arms crossed, waiting for an answer.

"Okay, I'll tell you, but you are not going to like what I am about to say."

"Everybody stop for a minute!"

Jake had shouted loud enough for Ben, now far ahead, to hear. He halted immediately as the words reached him, as did the other two men still under Jake's influence.

"All right, dog, now tell me."

"Uh…" The dog squirmed as he began to tell the tale. "The others before you were not actually related to you by blood, Jake. They were like you, similar in characteristics you might say. You are a descendant of one even greater, one feared by my kind from ancient times. He understood that your very existence would be challenged."

"A sect of followers, people who would do his bidding throughout time until you would arrive, became the handlers. They were given instruction to raise the others from birth until they came into their awareness. Then the texts would be harvested and kept safe until your arrival."

"What does that mean exactly?" Jake hoped it was not as it sounded.

"It means that the writings could not be allowed to fall into the hands of the evil ones. It was too great a risk to allow each of you to wander about with the possibility that you could be captured. Not long after each one would pass into the awareness, their handlers would harvest the skin. Each one was removed, dried, and rolled into a scroll."

"The handlers were to guard it until *your* arrival. You are the *one*, Jake, and we are here now because the guardian of this scroll had no choice but to hide it, likely perishing shortly thereafter, probably jumping to their death to avoid questioning."

"So you mean that the others were murdered by their own handlers after the text appeared on them?" Jake wasn't sure how to process this information, and he was beginning to feel quite anxious. "Are you going to kill me Pete? Is that why those people were at the apartment the night of my birthday?"

The dog laughed, "Don't be a fool. You are the *one* we all have been waiting for. They were there to help you. Besides, I am not powerful enough to kill you. You are growing stronger by the minute. Can't you feel it?"

Maire appeared to be in a state of shock. She had picked up a large stone halfway through Pete's story. If he had appeared to threaten Jake in any way, she was more than prepared to take action.

"So what's your plan then, dog?" she asked.

Pete turned to face her and saw the rock in her hands.

"What is this *then, girl?*" he mocked. "You were expecting to use that stone on me? How sweet, but unnecessary. You've seen what he can do. Do you think he needs your help?"

The conversation was taking the three of them away from the mission at hand and into a dark place.

"That's enough, you two." Jake was firm. "We can't continue to argue about what has happened in the past. We can only follow through with what we know right now. I say we get the scroll and get the hell out of here before something bad happens."

"But, Jake, how can we be sure now…"

"Forget about it, Maire."

He turned to Pete. "You should have told me this before. Is there anything else you haven't told me?"

"Uh, besides the fact that I actually, sort of, *like* you and want to help you succeed even if it means the end of my own existence? Nothing I can think of at this moment."

"Okay, then. Let's get going."

EIGHTEEN

As the group reached the peak of the mountain, they found the building where refreshments were available during the day when the park was open. Looking out across the land was breathtaking as so many lights lit up the night. The view of Atlanta's skyline was especially so.

"Ben, we've arrived. You can relax now." His voice swirled once again, as he released the man from his influence. "How are you feeling?"

"Huh? I feel good, but it sure is hot tonight. I'm sweating like a bull in a boiler room. Where are we?" The man was holding his headlamp band and mopping his brow with his shirt, which was pulled up to expose his hairy belly.

"We're at the top of Stone Mountain. I had to help you get up here, remember?"

"Uh, nope." He looked at Jake with a blank expression, "You mean I climbed up here on my own, or you dragged me?"

"He talked to you in that sexy voice of his and you almost ran to the top." Maire smiled. "You even asked if I wanted you to carry me."

"Magic, who knew?" He shook his head and walked toward the fence that surrounded the top of the mountain.

"Okay, let's get the ropes tied together and get on with this."

Jake walked over to the rangers who had sat down on the ground as Pete had ordered them. Retrieving the ropes, he began working on various knots and connectors while Pete and Maire joined Ben at the fence.

"It's a long way down. Do you think Jake will be able to retrieve the scroll and then get to the ground safely?" Maire bit her lip as she looked to Ben for some assurance. She couldn't bear the thought of Jake getting hurt. Worse, it was entirely possible that he could get himself killed.

"Trust me, young lady. That man of yours is ready for the task. I've seen him in action several times now. He certainly can handle himself." They watched as Jake continued to test his connections on the rope.

"I'm ready. Let's tie this rope off." Jake pointed out the support cable for the lift that was fastened into the rock. "This should be strong enough." Using a series of knots and carabiner clips, he attached the rope and uncoiled it as he walked to the fence.

"The moonlight makes it easy to see the park down there," she called to Jake. "Take a look."

He did not catch what she was saying. His mind was focused on the task at hand.

"All righty," he said. "I just have to throw this over the fence, and then I'll get myself over the edge of the rock and rappel down to the nostril of the horse. No problem."

He pulled a pair of fingerless gloves from his pocket and put them on. After adjusting the sheath of the knife he had affixed to his climbing belt, he grabbed a small rosin bag from his pouch and rubbed his hands together to coat them with the sticky powder.

Taking hold of the rope and clipping a carabiner to it, he leaned toward Maire.

"Can I get a kiss for luck?"

She met him full on the lips.

"No way am I kissing you," Pete complained.

Maire laughed into Jake's mouth as the kiss came to an abrupt end.

"Stupid dog," Jake grumbled. He turned and started climbing the fence.

Maire ran up behind him. "I love you, Jake. Be safe down there."

"You too, Maire."

He smiled and tossed the coils over the side. With the rope in both hands, he backed up to the edge, took a deep breath, and disappeared over the side. Once he found the scroll, he would rappel down the face of the mountain to the ground. The others would wait at the top until he signaled that he had the scroll before travelling back down the trail to get the truck and meet him in the parking lot.

NINETEEN

Somewhat nervous, Jake pushed away from the rock with his feet and dropped about ten feet closer to his destination. The rope held steady and he let it glide through his gloved hands as he descended. Around him, the quiet ambience of the night included the sounds of barking dogs and hooting owls. He thought the owls seemed unusually active, screeching and hooting to each other from the trees below.

He wasn't in a hurry to reach the carved face of the monument. Better to be safe than speedy. He hadn't done much rappelling before, so caution seemed the best strategy. He tried to not look down. The dizzying height affected him more than he had estimated from the ground. It wasn't long before he found a ledge below him, and he eased himself down onto it where he could relax for a moment and catch his breath.

Looking to his right, he made out the markings of the face of one of the soldiers. He hadn't realized he was so close. He was standing on the top of the horse's head with the rope that was to extend to the ground coiled at his feet. Carefully he gathered it onto his arm, making sure it was not tangled.

He lifted it up and threw it as hard as he could out and away from the mountain. He backed up to the edge to verify that the rope had fallen freely. As far as he could see into the shadows, it had not been caught again by any protrusion. It occurred to him that he should have chosen the day-glow green rope. It would have been easier to see by moonlight.

From where he stood, the ledge was wide enough for him to walk backward down the forehead of the horse to the muzzle and drop down to the nostril from there. As he began his descent, he thought about his friends waiting for him above. They had planned for him to signal his success by whipping the rope but now it seemed that would be impossible to accomplish.

Finally, he reached the end of the horse's nose. Pulling a rock pylon and hammer from a bag around his waist, he drove the metal spike into a crevice, hooked a carabiner into the ring on the end, and fed his rope through. He pulled hard on the pylon before deciding it was steady enough to begin lowering himself down.

At the lower rim of the nostril, he pushed himself back and swung inside. Immediately, he began to sense vibrations, a warm sensation. Assuming it was coming from the scroll, he carefully walked toward the wall and turned on his flashlight. He could see a well-stacked pile of flat stones inserted into an opening in the rock.

Shoving the sharp end of his hammer into the cracks between the stones, he pried the first one loose. The other stones fell away from the hole as he pulled the first one out. He jumped back to prevent his toes from being crushed. As he moved closer, the hole in the wall appeared to have been carved deep. He realized now that the glow he had seen before was probably his imagination playing tricks on him, because there was no glow except from the lamp on his headband.

He turned to look directly inside and the beam of his light fell across the prize. There was the scroll, intact and well preserved. Jake pulled a nylon bag with a string closure from his hip pack. He retrieved the scroll and placed it inside, pulling the rope tight to close it and tying it to his belt. "Time to go," he said as he gave the scroll a triumphant pat and he adjusted the rope for his descent to the ground.

Far above him, Maire was waiting for his signal. While he had climbed down the horse's face, there had been steady tension on the rope and she felt the vibrations of his movements, but once he had added the pylon, the vibrations had stopped.

She began to fret, "I don't feel him any more. Do you think something has gone wrong?"

Ben tried to calm her. "He's probably reached the scroll. If he's got solid footing, he will give himself some slack and you won't be able to feel his movement as much. My guess is that we'll be leaving here soon."

Pete, who had been keeping his eyes on the park rangers, moved toward the fence line. "Something is terribly wrong, I can feel it." He was barking loud enough for everyone to hear. "Ben, did you bring your spyglass?"

"You mean the binoculars? Yes, I did."

"Look down there and tell me what you see."

Ben fumbled with his hip pack and pulled out his compact night vision binoculars, holding them up to his eyes. At first, everything was blurred until he adjusted the wheel between his thumb and finger to focus and looked again, scanning the ground below.

"Holy shit, we are screwed! Signal Jake right away!"

"What do you see?" Maire grabbed the binoculars to have a look. "How do you work this?"

"There's a wheel in the middle; turn it until it clears up." Ben tried to help, but she pulled away and did it herself.

"Oh no! What are those people doing? Oh my god... they're ripping their skins off... it looks like they're... They ate their own skins!" Her voice had become shrill. "Oh my god... not human... We have to warn Jake!" she shrieked.

"Did you say they were eating their skin? Huskers!" Pete howled. "Those things can climb straight up a stone wall."

"What? What are huskers? What do you mean they can climb?" Maire was panicked since the dog had begun to howl.

"They are the worst kind of demons. They are the ones who killed Jake's handlers. They can easily climb straight up this mountain." Pete paced back and forth as he yelped, "Jake can't go down the way we planned. He must climb back up. We have to warn him."

There was no time to explain. Pete backed up and ran toward the fence. He nearly cleared the top as he leapt over to the other side, but caught his hind foot in the ragged fence top. He flipped mid-air and landed on his back a few feet from the drop-off.

"Pete!" Maire yelled. "What are you doing?"

"I'm fine," he barked back as he pulled himself up and shook himself off. Stepping right to the edge, he howled into the night.

"Climb up, Jake! Huskers coming! Climb UP!"

Jake backed up as far as he could and pushed out and away. He bounced about three times before feeling a jerk on the rope and then another. For a moment, he did not realize what was happening, but then he heard Pete howling.

"Huskers?"

Looking down below, he saw the lawn was crawling with people and others who were definitely not human. Some were beginning to climb the wall from below. It appeared that a half dozen of them were scrambling up the rope at an amazing speed while others were actually clinging to the stone and inching their way toward him.

The creatures emitted an eerie orange glow. The closer they got, the better he could make out their grotesque appearance. For a split second, he froze unable to move. Pete was yelling for him to climb up, but he didn't think that he could. His mind was scrambling for a solution until he remembered the knife on his belt.

As fast as he could, he climbed up the rope and back to the rim of the horse's nostril. Pulling himself up, he could hear the shrieking demons climbing up behind him. The rope made it far too easy for them to climb, and they were closing in fast, nearly thirty yards or less from the ledge where he was standing.

Swiftly, he pulled the knife from its sheath and cut the rope. He watched as it slipped over the edge and the demons went crashing down the face of the rock, knocking off the others who had been scrambling up beneath them. All of them slammed into to the ground below.

Did his eyes deceive him, or did they quickly get to their feet and start climbing again? He needed to get to the top before they could get to him. With fumbling fingers, he attached the dangling end of the rope to his harness and cinched it tight. He got to his feet and began to climb powered by a sudden surge of adrenalin.

He made his way to the top of the horse's face and the pylon he had left there. Unclipping the carabiner, he took a deep breath, and then ran to the top of the head dragging the slack of the rope behind him as he went.

When he reached the point where the rope was hanging straight down from above, he braced his feet and headed up the rock wall. Leaning back slightly, he put one foot in front of the other and pulled hand over hand toward the top.

"He's climbing; I can feel him." Maire turned to Ben. "We need to help. We have to pull him up. Pete, come back over the fence."

The dog turned to answer her, "There is not enough room to run." He stood at the edge watching the coming onslaught.

Maire and Ben were not making any progress pulling Jake up. They were going to need help. Maire yelled at Pete through the fence, "Get the rangers to help us, Pete. They look stronger than any of us."

Pete nodded and let his words swirl past Maire and Ben, sending them directly to the men. "Stand up and pull the rope. Pull it fast and pull it hard until the boy is up."

The two men came to life and jumped to their feet. Running to the fence, they grabbed the rope in front of Maire and Ben and began to pull the rope like cranking machines.

Some hundred and fifty feet below, Jake lost his footing as the rope jerked upward. He shot toward the top bouncing against the rock, his body scraping against the abrasive stone. Finally, he got his feet in front of him and nearly ran straight up the last fifty feet to the top. As he cleared the edge, the others were still pulling him across the ground toward the fence.

"Stop!" Pete barked.

The men dropped the rope into coils at their feet. Jake stood there blinking, catching his breath.

"Good job, guys. Now what?"

"Help me over that fence," Pete answered. "If you stand next to it, I can jump while you boost me over."

No further instruction was necessary. Jake quickly got into position and Pete galloped toward him. When he was close enough, he jumped and the boy lifted him higher as he flew over his shoulder. The dog landed on his feet on the other side of the fence while Jake scaled it and hopped to the ground below.

No sooner had he landed than Maire rushed over and threw her arms around him. "I thought they would surely get to you."

"They are still on their way. We need another plan."

He looked around the area for anything they could use as a weapon. As it was, all they had was his climbing hammer and knife.

"They're probably surrounding the mountain, so there's no clear way to get down now. I am afraid this could be the end of us." Pete had never sounded so defeated.

Ben spoke up, "How about a helicopter?"

"Are you crazy? Where are we going to get a helicopter, Ben?"

Ben pointed at the park rangers. "They have radios. They can call for an airlift. Tell them, Jake. We're injured hikers in need of emergency transport. We need help right now!"

"Damn good idea." Jake's voice changed as he gave the rangers the instructions. "Call for a helicopter. We need immediate assistance: several hikers have been injured and they need to be airlifted to a hospital. This is urgent, right away!"

One of the rangers held the radio to his mouth and repeated Jake's words even as they left his lips. He finished the broadcast command with, "Over and out!"

Ben roared. "Over and out?" He laughed so hard he was wheezing.

Maire was glaring at him. "This is no time to get hysterical, Professor. Those things are still climbing up to get us."

"I know, I know, but over and out? That's some ancient TV speak if I ever heard it," he gasped.

Jake looked back through the fence at the ledge. "Grab whatever you can find to throw at those creatures when they come over the top. We might be able to knock them off at least."

"I don't see anything, Jake." Maire was looking around.

Pete was thinking. "Jake, there's something we haven't tried. You know how the marks on your hands and your left foot give you some special ability to deal with the demons, but there is also a mark on your right foot. Maybe it's true…"

"What do you know, dog? Spit it out!"

"I've never seen it myself, but I have heard of the wave of fire. Something you are supposed to have the ability to do. The others I have helped never had the chance to try it. Supposedly…"

With the sound of a helicopter heading their way, Jake asked, "How does it work?"

"I have no idea. I just know that if I am in the area, it will kill me as well as all the others." Pete's ears drooped.

"What if you are over the ridge when I do it, whatever *it* is. Do you think it will miss you then?"

"Jake, if the helicopter doesn't arrive in time, you will have no choice. Just do it. Keep in mind that you can only do it once every few days. My understanding is that it will drain you…"

Jake raised his voice above the increasing noise of the approaching helicopter. "Okay then, what do I do? Aim my foot at them and concentrate? Do I have to take off my shoe? What?"

"I'm trying to recall. It's been hundreds of years since…"

The shrieking of huskers coming up to the top of the mountain was loud enough now to compete with the sound of the helicopter.

"I believe you must remove your shoe or it will be destroyed. Wait until the very last moment, then bring the palms of your hands together and stomp down hard with the foot. Every one of my kind in your line of sight will be destroyed. At least I think that's how…"

"Run then, my friend. Once I've done this get back here as fast as you can. I won't leave without you, I promise."

"But Jake…"

"Go now. Run!"

He sat down and began to unlace his hiking boot as Pete turned and ran as fast as he could go.

"Good luck, my friends," he barked as he disappeared over the ridge.

Maire felt helpless as she watched the only one who really knew anything at all about the strange creatures coming toward them run off into the night. She crouched down next to Jake as he pulled his boot from his foot and helped him stand to face the cliff ahead of them. In the distance, they could see the lights of the approaching helicopter as the first gnarled heads of a dozen huskers appeared over the edge of the cliff.

RUNE

Episode IV: Entombed

ONE

"What are they waiting for?" Maire clung to Jake's arm as the horde of huskers continued to climb up over the edge and inch their way to the fence, the only obstacle standing between them and the onslaught.

"I think they're waiting to gather a greater and more powerful force before they attack. That's exactly what I would do if I were facing an unknown opponent. I'd want as many of them as possible to get up here before I take them out."

Jake felt a twinge in his gut as he looked over at Maire. She was looking back at him expectantly, her hair blowing in the breeze, when the thought occurred to him. *What if this thing doesn't work?* The huskers were after the skin from his back, and they would have to kill him to get it. If Maire and Ben were fighting next to him, and the plan failed, they would be ripped apart.

"Maire, listen." He reached for her hand. "Go with Ben. Head that way, the way that Pete went. If anything goes wrong, you'll have a chance to escape, and..." He swallowed hard as he choked out the words, "If something happens to me, if I die, promise me you'll kick Pete's ass for getting us involved in this in the first place."

"But you can't fight them off alone if your plan doesn't work." She looked at Jake and then over his shoulder.

The creatures were amassing on the other side of a fence that did not appear to offer much security in the face of such a force. She began to feel her panic rising. Jake, keenly aware that the demons were swarming up and over the edge of the rock, gave her a slight nudge. The front line was tightly pressed against the fence, and the last of the open space behind them was nearly filled.

"No time to argue, Maire. Ben, take her and run," Jake yelled to his friend who seemed mesmerized by the creatures intent on taking their prize at any cost.

Ben took hold of Maire's arm and pulled her back toward the trail they had used earlier. Tears streaming, she followed, leaving Jake to stand alone. One shoe on and one shoe off, he would face the demon army from hell.

Although the boy's mind was focused, he felt queasy as he prepared himself for the charge. The force coming against him would be so powerful that it would surely consume him if this plan should fail. His heart was heart racing, beating loudly in his ears as though it would pound its way out of his chest.

The creatures waiting on the rock remained silent as though waiting for some signal to strike. Those still climbing shrieked and snarled in a state of frenzy as they made their way to the top, pushing forward to join the others.

"How many of you bastards are there?" Jake challenged them as their flaming eyes focused on his every twitch. "You better get 'em all up here before you…"

A bone-piercing howl cut off his tirade. Up and over the fence they came, swarming like ants. The fence leaned toward him as it began to collapse under their weight. Jake prepared for impact, but was surprised when they didn't come straight for him. Instead, they kept a distance of fifteen feet or more away, and began to circle around him. He could smell their foul breath even from a distance, and the sounds they made chilled the blood in his veins.

He let his arms hang loose at his sides in order to appear vulnerable, as though he were simply waiting for death. As they closed the gap to surround him, he brought his hands up in front of him, palms inward and ready. Quietly under his breath, he whispered, "Wait. Wait. Wait."

The fence had come all the way down, as the last of the creatures made their way to the top of the mountain and took their place in the circle. When all were assembled, they rushed him from all sides.

"Now you die!" Jake yelled as he clapped his hands together. He lifted his naked foot and stomped down hard against the mountain. A flash of fear ran through him when nothing seemed to happen. The demons slammed into his body, clawing and slashing at him mercilessly. Jake screamed in agony as their sharp talons ripped his clothes and tore at his flesh.

Then he felt it. An updraft of air began swirling around him from the ground below his feet as a column of blue fire rose up around him. Any creature within arm's distance exploded into flames. Like a magician's flash paper, they were gone.

It did not keep the demons from charging, and as they moved against him, they too were destroyed. Jake was feeling weak as his injured body tried to heal itself. He waited for the *wave* of fire that Pete had described, but there was no indication that the fiery blue column would spread out horizontally. Instead, it shot straight up into the sky.

Unsure how much longer he could sustain the drain on his energy, he desperately weighed his options for escape. If he gave out before the helicopter could land, it would likely be the end of it all. His thoughts had distracted him. Too late, he realized that he had allowed the palms of his hands to separate.

The flames fell at his feet. For a split second, all hope drained from his body, only to revive as the wave of blue destruction washed out over the surface of the rocky mountaintop, vaporizing row after row of the bloodthirsty huskers in a massive succession of flame, spark, and ash. Looking down now, he was amazed to learn that the flame could be controlled by the movement of his hands.

TWO

Moments before the demons launched their attack, a large search and rescue chopper was nearing its destination at the top of Stone Mountain. There had been a report of injured hikers, but as they approached the scene below, they could see that a massive attack was underway. Hundreds of people were fanned out around the base of the mountain and more were streaming out from the woods to join them.

"What the hell is this?" the paramedic yelled into his microphone as they came within sight of the mountaintop. One man stood alone in an open area surrounded by a crowd of strange-looking people. Something was wrong.

"That man is…" the pilot yelled back through the microphone on his helmet. "We can't land in that… what the fu…!"

Out of nowhere, a brilliant blue column of flame shot into the sky. As they circled the scene, there were small explosions at the base of the flame, and then it fell back to the ground. In an instant, the blue fire spread out across the surface of the rock and fiery debris blew right off the side of the mountain. When the blast was gone, the horde that had surrounded the man had vanished. The lights on the control panel of the chopper were flickering and it seemed as though the engines were about to fail.

"Did you feel that?" The co-pilot moaned as the last glimmer of the shockwave passed through the helicopter. The chopper had quickly recovered and the spinning blades lifted the aircraft higher. "Damn, I feel so warm and…"

"Oh man, it felt like… love or something. I felt it too. Like we just took part in some kind of gigantic group hug!" The paramedic clutched at his chest as if to keep it from bursting. He pointed at Jake who now stood alone on the rock. "Look, all of those freaky-looking people are gone."

The pilot moved the control stick to the right. "Let's get down there and find out what the hell just happened." He brought the chopper down on a flat spot to Jake's left as the shreds of his torn clothes flapped wildly from the wind they had created.

THREE

By the time the helicopter powered down enough for the paramedic to climb out, Ben and Maire were at Jake's side. They were looking him over and trying to figure how they could help him with the insane volume of slash wounds he had sustained.

"I'm okay, I just need to sit down." Jake could see the tears on their faces as they checked the shreds of his bloody clothes and the skin that hung from his arms. "It looks worse than it is."

"It looks pretty bad, Jake. That has to hurt." Ben's hands hovered near the young man, and he reached out to help steady him.

Jake could feel his body beginning to heal as they eased him to the ground. Quickly, Maire turned and ran toward the helicopter as it settled to the ground. She waved her arms and pleaded for help though her words were masked by the noise from the spinning blades.

The side door slid open and a man carrying a first aid kit jumped out and headed toward Jake. Maire slowed her pace. The medic hadn't been able to hear what she was saying, but as soon as he had stepped out of the chopper, he could see the bloody, injured man sitting on the ground.

"Don't worry, miss, we'll get him out of here and to the hospital straight away." Maire could see his mouth moving, but it was still too loud to hear. She turned to lead him to Jake. By the time they reached the injured boy, he was attempting to get to his feet.

"Sit down, fella, and let me look at those wounds. We'll get you out of here ASAP." He knelt, opening his kit and moving some items around before pulling out a roll of gauze and some large bandages. "I hate to ask too many questions, but what in the world just happened up here?"

Jake said nothing, only watching as the man went about his business. When it seemed the paramedic was about to examine him further, he spoke in a deep fluid voice that floated above the noise. "You will take us to our truck, me and my friends. All of them."

"I'll take you to your truck. Where is it?" The man's voice was a hollow monotone.

"In the parking lot at the head of the trail." Jake could feel the gashes on his arms closing. "Give me your shirt, sir."

The man did as he was asked. He unbuttoned and removed his shirt, handing it to Jake.

"The undershirt, please. Hurry!" He turned to look around and yelled, "Pete, where are you?"

"He's coming, Jake," Maire assured him. "He's checking over the ledge to see what's coming next."

Jake tore away the bloody remains of his shredded shirt. He took the white t-shirt from the man and wiped most of the blood from his body. It had completely healed by now and showed no sign of injury. He put on the paramedic's uniform shirt and buttoned it halfway up.

"Everybody to the chopper!" Pete barked as he ran toward the group. "There's another wave of huskers climbing up the rock. You won't be able to use that fire trick again for a while, Jake. We'll all die here if we don't get moving."

"Let's get to the chopper, everybody. Move!" Jake ordered. Everyone ran for the helicopter, including the park guards, who had been standing quietly nearby, waiting to be told what to do.

As Ben and Pete climbed in, the pilot began to protest, "Hey, you all can't fit in here. I won't be able to lift off with all of you and the equipment."

Pete's low, controlling growl swirled sweetly around the cockpit while Jake ordered the paramedic to throw all of the equipment overboard. Without question, the man obeyed.

"You will sit here and wait until my friends are aboard, and then you will fly us away," Pete commanded the pilot who was getting out of his seat to stop his partner from throwing out all of the medical equipment.

Ben and Jake waited as the rest of the group climbed aboard the emptied shell of the helicopter. As Maire was settling in, she glanced out the window, her heart stopping as she glimpsed the heads of huskers popping up over the edge of the rock.

"They're coming!" she yelled, croaking, barely getting the words out as the panic rose in her throat.

Jake and Pete were just closing the door behind them when the pilot took off unannounced. The engines roared as he gave it full throttle. Everyone held their breath when it seemed they would not be able to lift off, but the chopper began to rise. Hordes of huskers were rushing over the crushed fence as the altitude between the rock and the chopper slowly increased.

The demons screamed and made a run for it, leaping into the air, grasping for anything they could reach. A couple of the most determined caught hold of the landing gear and while the chopper gained altitude, they scrambled up and began pounding on the closed door. When they tried to pry it open, Jake became alarmed.

"Let me at the door!" Jake was literally climbing over the others to get to the door. Just then, the determined huskers managed to move the door, trying to force their way in.

Jake braced himself and slapped them on the head with the palms of both hands. He was surprised when they both went limp and fell from the side of the chopper like a pair of toy dolls, slamming into the rock below. It was clear to him now that these creatures were not possessed by demons. They *were* demons.

"Take us down to our truck," he commanded the pilot, pointing, "It's the black one right there."

FOUR

When the overstuffed helicopter touched down in the parking lot, there was no one else in sight. Jake ordered everyone out, and one by one, the passengers stepped out onto the pavement. As the paramedic and pilot followed, Jake asked, "Where are you going?" He held out his arm to block them. "Get back in the chopper and fly back to your base. When you arrive, you will remember nothing that has happened here." The pair turned and climbed back in as ordered. When everyone on the ground was clear of the blades, the chopper took off straightaway.

It was time to exit this place, and Jake gave the park rangers their orders. "Get in your truck and lead us to the highway. Don't stop for anyone or anything. When we are safely on our way, you will drive to the nearest gas station and go into the restroom. You will wake with no recollection of what has happened here this day."

The two rangers ran for their truck and the team headed for theirs. "I'll drive," Ben volunteered as he pressed the button on the remote key.

"Good idea, I feel a little shaky. I'll ride shotgun this time, Pete." Jake grabbed the handle of the front passenger door.

No sooner had everyone climbed into the truck, than the crowds of possessed people who had been encircling the base of the mountain came around the bend from both directions.

"This doesn't look good for us," Pete growled. "We'll have to drive through them to escape this place."

"Which is exactly the reason we got the Beast in the first place. Lock your doors, everybody, here we go!" Ben hit the gas and fell in behind the park rangers' truck, which was moving fast toward the park's exit gate.

"Oh God, I can't watch this." Maire put her head down and covered her eyes as the rangers' truck plowed into the oncoming horde of screaming people.

Most of the crowd separated as the rangers cleared the way, but here and there, one of them would make a dash to intercept them. The Beast rolled right over them with a thumping, crunching sound that caused the passengers inside to cringe and groan with empathy for the poor souls who were falling in their path.

Ahead, Ben could see the gates. The rangers continued to roll on through, but the crowd was not thinning. As the pickup plowed along, people were falling beneath the wheels and bouncing off the sides.

"How far to the highway?" Maire yelled as she squeezed her eyes shut and covered her ears to muffle the shrieks and screams of those they were running down.

"A quarter mile or so," Ben yelled back to her. "I'm not sure if we're going to make it. There are hundreds of people blocking the road ahead."

"Go off road, Ben. Engage the four-wheel like the salesman showed you." Jake's suggestion was just in time as the rangers' truck plowed into a wall of people and ground to a halt.

Ben shifted the truck into four-wheel drive, swerving to the right and off the road. As they drove into the tall grass, the last thing Jake could see were the two rangers being dragged from the cab of their truck. *I hope they make it out alive*, he thought, as he bounced on the seat. The ride was rougher than he expected, and he wondered if Maire had buckled her seat belt.

Ben roared with a combination of maniacal laughter and screams as he maneuvered past the throng of possessed who were attempting to pursue them into the field. To his left he could see that the road was clear, and he cut the wheel to get back to it. The Beast obediently bounced back up onto the pavement. Ben gunned the engine and they merged onto the highway ramp headed toward Atlanta.

"Is everyone okay?" Jake asked, turning around to check Maire for injuries. The look on Pete's face answered the question.

"I have to admit, Jake. You certainly have a way of keeping things exciting. Have you always been this way, or am I somehow responsible?"

"You kidding me, dog?" He wanted to smack him. "Before you came along, the most exciting thing that I had going on was a promise from Maire in a birthday card."

"I thought you'd forgotten that." Maire's eyes were reddened and filled with tears.

"Not forgotten. Never forgotten. Just waiting for the right time and place. Like some time when there isn't a crowd of demon-possessed people trying to kill us and such." He unbuckled his seat belt and leaned into the space between the seats to put his hand on her shoulder. He pulled her toward him and kissed her on the forehead. "Hopefully, we'll live to see that."

"I hate to interrupt, but where are we headed next, boss?" Ben looked in the mirror at the two of them.

"Find a place to pull over, I need to check the book..." Jake reached down behind the seat and pulled the bag from the floor. He checked inside to make sure the book and two scrolls were still there. "We need to find a spray off car wash too. This truck could attract a lot of unwanted attention after all of that."

FIVE

In the back of the plaza, away from the other cars in the parking lot, Jake switched places with Pete. Sitting next to Maire in the back seat, he pulled the small golden knife from its pocket in the cover of the book.

"Don't look," he warned as he sliced deep into his hand. His blood landed on the center of the page and flowed through the veins lining each leaf of strange parchment. The writing began to appear.

"You've lost a lot of blood, Jake. Are you feeling all right? I hate that you have to do that each time you need to read that horrid book."

"You better get used to it, girl. We have four more scrolls to find before this party really gets interesting." Pete had grown tired of the frivolous concerns of this female. "This is the only way to get the information, and no one else is able to provide the ink. Ben has tried it before and the book didn't appreciate his attempt."

"Girl? Is that what you called me? Look, *Dog*, at least have the courtesy to call me by name. As far as I'm concerned, you have played a part in all this. If you and your demon-kind would have stayed in your own world, we wouldn't be going through any of this." Maire was reaching her breaking point.

Jake listened to the exchange between the two of them, but couldn't decide which side he was on. Instead, he changed the subject. "There's a new map here. I'm guessing it's the next location that we have to..."

Maire was glaring at him.

"What?" One look at her and he was sure that he was about to be drawn into the skirmish. He was right.

"He's your dog, er... friend. I don't care if he *is* possessed by some ancient demon. He needs to learn to address people by name, and not with scandalous tones of disrespect."

"Oh, geez. Open the door for me, Ben." Pete scowled as he leaned toward the door. "This dog needs to relieve himself and it's way too tempting to aim for the back seat right now."

"You aren't going to run off are you?" Ben was seriously concerned that they would not be able to complete this mission without the dog. He wasn't going to allow an easy escape if that was Pete's plan.

"Look, teacher, I have been through battles that have cost thousands of lives and spilled the blood of many innocents. I've seen the tyranny of torture and starvation in this world as I waited for this *one* young man to come of age. It will take more than the threats of a young *Maire* to dissuade me. Now, please, open the door."

Ben got out of the truck and walked around to open the door while Jake tried to return his focus back to the book.

"Maire, can you grab my phone out of the door compartment? We need to search for the meaning of these numbers."

Ben stood outside the truck and waited as the dog wandered over to the grass to find a suitable place to relieve itself.

"Ready?" Jake asked Maire as she woke up the phone.

"Go."

"29.9667N, 90.0500W. Let's see what it says." He waited for her response.

"It's New Orleans, Louisiana. Is that the next place we will have to go? Every year during Mardi Gras, I've always wondered what it was like there." She tried to contain her excitement, but her eyes were sparkling.

Jake was about to remind her that this was going to be no vacation, when Ben opened the door to let Pete back in the truck. "So where are we headed this time?"

"New Orleans. How far is that from here, do you think?" Jake asked.

"It's about 493 miles from here, depending on exactly where we need to be in that city." Maire was looking at the route on the phone.

"I was afraid it was going to be some place like that." Ben climbed into the driver's seat. "I've been there before for Mardi Gras. If any one place in the country could be loaded with demons, I'd say *that* is the one. They have a long history of voodoo and black magic there."

"I think we need to go somewhere safe first and let Jake rest. He needs to recharge before we run right into the next conflict," Pete advised.

Jake had caught on to his habit of holding back facts. "So why do I need to recharge? I admit I'm a little tired, but I feel okay considering what I've just been through."

"Because, my friend, if we encounter an army of huskers such as we did on that mountain, you will not be able to stop them. You must allow your power to build up again. You may feel well at the moment, but in a few hours, you are going to collapse from the drain on your energy."

"Then we should drive until we get out of the city before we find a motel. We can stay there until morning. Jake can get his rest, and we can shop for some clothes. Unless you think he should walk around in a paramedic's shirt and some half shredded pants." With the heat she had been taking from the dog, Maire had decided to think carefully before suggesting anything that might cause some kind of backlash. She was sure her plan was a good one.

"The Maire has a point."

"Pete," Maire sighed. "When the sentence calls for actually using the word *girl*, or any other reference to me, please feel free to use it. Just don't use it instead of my name when you address me directly. It's disrespectful."

The dog didn't bother to respond. Actually, he was genuinely confused. How was he supposed to know what this female expected from him in any given situation? He turned to face the window as Ben pulled out of the parking lot.

SIX

In all of Paris, every crow sitting on any rooftop or wire cringed. Their feathers ruffled as the demon queen screamed from her balcony. Trembling, they waited to be summoned, fearing they would be blamed for the debacle at the mountain. They had been made aware that throngs of minions who had stormed the mountain had been eradicated by some trick of the boy. Someone would surely have to pay.

It wasn't long before the call came.

Quickly, the birds settled onto the balcony with the largest one choosing the highest perch atop a column. From there, he looked down on Seraphine.

"Yes, Mistress, you summoned us?"

"By now, I am certain that you have heard the news about the utter failure of my servants in America. Yes?"

The bird nodded in response.

"And you are also aware that the one I am seeking is on the move once more?"

"Yes, Mistress. We anticipated the movement when our brethren saw what happened there."

Seraphine began to raise her hand, but the crow interrupted her quickly before she had a chance to strike him dead.

"It is the reason we have continued to follow them and can report that they are headed away from Atlanta going south and to the west."

Her fingers curled as she lowered her hand again. "So you are able to keep me apprised of their whereabouts? And, if I travel there, you have an agent that can advise me?"

"Yes, Mistress, we will have one of ours there to report on their progress when you arrive. It is an honor to serve you." The crow's heart was pounding within his breast. It seemed he had averted death, at least for the moment.

"So be it. We will leave at sunrise tomorrow morning. I will expect your counterpart to give me a report of the boy's location as soon as I set foot on solid ground. I suggest you relay that message."

"Yes, yes, you can be sure of it." The crow was grateful that the encounter had gone so well, however his relief would be short lived.

Seraphine extended her arms outstretched at her sides and snapped her fingers. Five of the lesser crows surrounding him exploded in a cloud of red mist and black feathers that settled to the stone floor of the balcony.

"Any failure to deliver on your promise will result in the same fate for you and the rest of your *brethren* within my reach." She bent over and picked up a feather that lay at her feet and examined it on her open palm before exhaling to blow it straight at him. "And be warned, my friend, my reach is immeasurable. Go now. You may make your arrangements."

For a moment, the crow stared down at the feathers and blood spattered below. He cawed furiously to signal the flock before silently opening his wings to fly from the balcony. What remained of his life's mate lay behind on the cold stone floor. As he led the others away, he vowed in his heart to exact some treachery on the beast of a woman who had caused him such pain and grief.

SEVEN

Jake sat with Pete in the room of the motel watching a movie from the rental list they had found next to the television. Maire and Ben had gone to the nearest shopping mall to get some new clothes for them all and cell phones for themselves.

Maire had protested that she already owned a phone, but Jake insisted that she upgrade in order to have all the available features. Ben had left his behind at his house in the rush and chaos as they began their journey, and there had been no way to go back for it. In fact, at this point Jake wondered if Ben would ever be able to return home. If their mission failed, home would not be the same for anyone on earth.

***

"Failure is not an option," Ben muttered through clenched teeth as he cruised the parking lot of the shopping center looking for a space near the door.

"What was that, Ben?" Maire inquired, pointing toward a vacant space. "Over there."

Steering into the space, he elaborated on his cryptic remark. "I was just thinking about the possible outcome of this mission we're on. What would become of us if something should happen to Jake, or even Pete?"

He turned off the engine and pulled the keys from the ignition. "When we were back at my house, I don't think I fully understood the implications of what we were about to do. Now, after what happened at the mountain, I realize that if we fail we will be in for a world of hurt the likes of which most people could never even imagine. Or, for that matter, survive."

"I was hoping that wasn't what you meant. I don't want to think about that right now." She opened the door and began to climb out of the truck, but turned back to Ben. "I honestly believe Jake knows what he's doing. He'll get us through this. I know he will." She stepped down on the pavement and slammed the door. "Right now, I need a happy moment free of this crap. Let's go shopping!"

***

Jake sat on the edge of the bed with his back toward the window. "I don't know where we are going to end up, Pete. The book only gives us bits of information at a time. There's no way to make any real plan."

"I believe there is a reason for that." Pete kept his eyes on the television as he softly barked, "If something happened, let's say you were captured, you could be coerced to reveal the locations of the remaining scrolls. Since the book only tells you a little at a time about the next one, there would be no way to extract the locations of the rest from you. The Invert needs those scrolls as much as we do."

"So… in other words, no matter how much I was tortured, I couldn't tell anyone where they were. No matter how much pain I endured."

"That is correct."

"Somehow, I don't find that to be comforting in the least. Let's just watch the movie. I need to clear my head."

"Of course, my friend. I want to see how this story will end anyway."

"My story?"

"No, the one we're watching over there." Pete lay on the bed facing the television and rested his head on his paws.

***

Maire was checking out a pair of jeans marked with Jake's size. She picked up another one marked "relaxed fit" to compare with the slimmer ones. After holding them side-by-side, she chose the slim jeans, taking every pair of that size and style from the rack and carrying them to the counter.

Ben stood in the fitting room and frowned at his reflection in the mirror. He hated shopping for clothes. Nothing ever seemed to fit the way he expected. Sure, it looked great on the mannequin, but when he put it on, it was always too tight or loose in all the wrong places. After some time, he emerged with three complete shirt and slacks combos. He was ready to go.

By then, Maire was no longer in the men's department. She had gone to find some outfits for herself. The store had no shopping carts, so Ben decided to take his items to the counter until she was ready to check out. She had the cash that Jake had told them to use, so he was going to have to wait for her anyway.

At the counter, he was surprised to find a mountain of jeans, shirts, underwear and socks piled high around the register. He assumed that the clothes were meant for Jake, so he cleared a spot for his own. After searching half the store, he found Maire with an armful of clothes heading for the fitting room.

"Hey, Maire." He caught up to her just before she disappeared through the doorway. "Was that pile of clothes at the register for Jake?"

"Yeah, I figure the way things are going we won't have time to do laundry. Don't you think? We can't wash shredded clothes anyway."

"I hadn't even thought of that. Maybe I need to grab a few more things then. I'll meet you back over at the counter when you're ready."

Maire disappeared through the door of the fitting room as he headed back to the dreaded rack. She seemed to be enjoying herself for the first time since they had left home. He shook his head. As intelligent as he was, he could never figure out the obvious difference between men and women when it came to shopping for clothes.

How could women enjoy it so much, and why did they take so long to choose something? He, and most other men he knew, only shopped for clothes when the old ones wore out. When it became necessary to replace them, they walked right in, picked something out, and paid for it. Done.

Finally, he decided that this wasn't the time or place to solve the mysteries of the universe. He grabbed a few more of the same shirts and slacks he had selected previously and went back to the counter to wait.

EIGHT

"I wonder why they are taking so long."

Pete was standing on his hind legs at the window with his nose pushed between the closed curtains. He had been pacing back and forth at the foot of the bed until Jake complained that it was making it difficult for him to see the television.

"Obviously, you have never been shopping with a woman before." Jake laughed.

"What does that mean? Why is shopping with a woman any different from doing so with a man? How odd you humans are."

"Most women can shop all day. In fact, some even rent buses and travel to large shopping centers where they can shop for an entire weekend."

"I don't see the attraction..." Pete hesitated and then announced, "The shoppers have returned."

Maire and Ben carried a single bag each when they came through the door. "Here, Jake. Get dressed. I think Ben wants to shower before he changes clothes. When everyone is ready, we can get back on the road."

She handed him the bag and flopped down on the bed. Ben was already removing the tags from his new clothes: a pair of jeans and a button down shirt, quite similar to the one he had been wearing.

"I hate shopping for clothes. I can never find anything I like, so I always end up with the same thing."

"I thought that shirt looked familiar," Jake smiled. "Didn't Maire say she was gonna get a couple of outfits since we can't do laundry?"

Ben guffawed. Catching his breath, he answered, "Wait until you see the back of the truck. It is filled with bags. Maire nearly emptied out the place of jeans your size."

"Well, look at what he has on! They're shredded. Dirty can be washed, but shredded is trash. You'll be glad I got as many as I did in a few days."

Jake interrupted, "It's okay, Maire. We have a long way to go before we can take time out for laundry. It's been a while since I had a new pair of jeans. A couple of them will be nice to have."

"How about twenty?" Ben snickered.

"I didn't know you were counting," Maire glared at the professor. "Besides, you're wrong." She leaned back on the bed and crossed her arms on her chest.

"How much longer before we get going?" Pete was getting antsy now. "I sense it is time to move on before we get trapped here. They are bound to catch up with us."

Jake appreciated the way that Pete could change the subject before the conversation spiraled into an argument. Not only that, the dog was usually right and this time for sure. They had been there too long already. If someone or something was tracking them, the forces of evil were likely already being assembled for the next assault.

"Get it going, Ben. Pete's right, we need to get out of here." He opened his bag and started removing the tags from his new jeans.

NINE

Ben was back behind the steering wheel, about an hour south of Montgomery, Alabama, when he spotted a motorcycle in the rearview mirror. The biker was a rough looking character with a graying beard and long scraggly hair that stuck out from under his helmet. Ben sped up and then slowed down to verify that the bike was pacing them at a consistent distance. Yes, they were being stalked.

"I think we might have a problem," he said as he adjusted the side mirror. "That guy on the motorcycle behind us seems to be following us. Either of you guys sensing anything?" He turned the rearview mirror to check Jake's face for signs of concern.

"Maybe, but I'm not sure I can judge a threat when we're moving like this." Pete looked in the mirror on his side of the truck.

Jake turned around to see for himself, but his view was obstructed by shopping bags. Pete pressed his paw on the power window button and rolled it all the way down so he could stick his head out. His ears flapped as he sniffed the air blowing past him. To anyone outside the vehicle, he would appear just as any other dog enjoying the wind. However, Pete was not finding it to be enjoyable at all. Finally, he pulled his head in and rolled the window back up.

"I couldn't smell a thing, but that guy looks like trouble, and there are more behind him."

As they passed the next on-ramp for merging traffic, Jake groaned. There was a line of motorcycles pouring onto the freeway as they passed.

"Ben, step on it. I think his whole gang just figured out where we are."

The professor pressed his foot against the accelerator and began to move ahead of the bikers, but there was no shaking them. They sped up to keep pace with the truck. By the time the last bike had fallen in behind them, Ben was already pushing over 85 mph. He tightened his grip on the steering wheel when several bikers pulled up alongside his door and started banging on the truck with their fists.

"How the hell can they do that without crashing? We're going almost 90 now. I'm having trouble keeping *this* thing on the road. We need to do something or they're going to run us off the road."

When the truck came upon and passed another car travelling in the fast lane, the bikers fell back behind them. As soon as they had passed it, they quickly began moving up again.

"Hand me a bag of those clothes, Maire." Jake was rolling down the window.

She hesitated. She had put a lot of thought into selecting those clothes. Was he was going to throw them out the window?

"Maire… never mind." Jake reached over the back of the seat and grabbed a bag. "Let them get a little closer to my window, Ben," Jake yelled over the howling wind rushing in the window. He fumbled with one of the shirts. It was folded and pinned to a piece of thin cardboard. "This looks like Ben's shirt."

"Aw, man! You're going to throw my shirt out the window?" The truck jerked as he tried to see in the mirror which shirt Jake had in his hand.

"Just drive! I don't have time to be selective here."

Jake pulled the pins from the shirt as one of the bikers moved into position near his window. He stretched his arm out into the wind and let the shirt fly. It opened up like a parachute and sailed right past the first biker to wrap around the face of the guy behind him. The lead biker hit the brakes to slow, but the other one couldn't see and plowed into his rear fender, pushing the bike sideways. Rubber caught the road and both of them began to flip.

Pete marveled at the sight of the two motorcycles tumbling down the road, arms and legs flying as the riders slammed repeatedly against the pavement. The rest of the gang swerved to miss them, but three more went down before they could recover and continue the chase. At such a high rate of speed, it was doubtful that anyone involved in the wreck could survive it.

"Jake, what's that person holding?" The dog was fixated on a reflection of light coming from the biker's hand as he moved up to close the distance between them. The truck swerved again as Ben tried to see what Pete was looking at.

Maire called out, "He has a piece of metal chain!"

"Faster, Ben. This is about to get out of control." Jake leaned forward and glanced at the speedometer. It was already registering 92 mph.

"It was out of control the moment it started. Everybody check your seatbelts," Ben yelled as he pushed the pedal to the floor.

The truck shot away, and Jake checked the speedometer again. He was alarmed to discover that they were inching toward 115. His pulse quickened even more when he looked at the mirror and saw the look of absolute terror on the older man's face. Up ahead, they were about to reach a bridge over the highway and it gave him an idea.

"The next time we are headed under a bridge like this one, stop and let me out. Whether there's an exit there or not. I need you to drop me off, and then get on it up above me and wait." He hoped Ben would understand what he meant because there was no time to explain.

"What are you going to do? Don't sacrifice yourself for…"

"They won't follow you if you let me out. They're after me. So let them think they've got me. Here comes the next underpass. Get ready to drop me off. Don't worry, I have a plan."

Ten

Smoke rolled up from the tires as Ben locked up the brakes. He knew better than to argue with the boy. After all, he had the ability to control him at will with his hypnotic voice. He understood that as soon as the truck skidded to a stop, Jake was going to jump out. The only thing to do was exactly what he had been told. Get to the top of the bridge and wait.

The bikers had been outdistanced by more than a mile, but they were catching up quickly. Jake knew he had to act fast. Before the truck came to a full stop, he had the door open and was out.

"Go!" he yelled.

Ben floored the accelerator and cut the wheel as soon as they exited the other side of the bridge. The truck bounced over a small rise and slammed into a chain link fence, which snapped and fell beneath the weight of the truck. They powered over it and headed up the bank.

"Ben! They're going to tear him apart! Why did you agree to this crazy idea?" Maire was frantic as they left Jake behind.

Ben stayed focused on getting them to the top of the bridge, while Pete and Maire strained to see what Jake was going to do.

"I think he's going to use the wave of fire," Pete howled, "but I don't know if he has had enough time to recover from the last time. It might not work."

"What? Why didn't you stop him?" Maire was more than panicked now.

"For the same reason that Ben did as he was told. If we stay down at road to try to reason with him, the wave would kill me the same as it will the rest of my kind. This way, he can target the ones that are controlling those bikers. You must know by now that Jake is not the same boy he was just days ago. He knows what he's doing, and up to this point, his choices have been spot-on."

As the truck rolled midway across the bridge, Maire countered, "None of that makes this any easier."

Truth be told, she secretly admired his new courage and strength. In every situation they had encountered, he had grown in her estimation. She was more enamored with him than ever.

When the truck came to a stop, Ben threw open the door and jumped out of the truck. He could hear the roar of the motorcycles in the distance, but he wanted to see what would happen when they caught up with Jake. Bending over the railing, he could see Jake standing there holding his shoe. He was backing up beneath the bridge and out of view.

With a jolt, Ben remembered the swords they had packed in the truck. He turned and ran for the open door, thrusting his hand under the seat. Maire trembled as the tips of the sheaths disappeared under the seat in front of her.

"Wait here. If this doesn't work, he's going to need help." he told her as he pulled out the swords. He ran back to the railing of the bridge. The bikers were closing in on Jake, slowing as they prepared to dismount, but Ben couldn't see much of what was going on directly below him.

The high-pitched shrieks of the bikers rose above the rumbling sounds of their engines. Their orders were to take the skin from the boy's back, but the rest of his body was theirs to do with as they wished. At this moment, what they wished was to eat him alive and savor his suffering. They revved their engines and taunted their prey.

Ben had no idea what to expect since he couldn't see Jake at all. When the wave of blue flame hit the crazed bikers, it was as much of a surprise to him as it was to them. Suddenly, the area was filled with a reverberating boom as the blast of the wave blew out from under the bridge. Ben dropped the swords to cover his ears.

He stood helplessly fascinated as the demons were blown out of the bodies of the bikers and sent flaming into the faces of the next thug behind. One by one, the liberated bodies of the bikers collapsed to the ground. They fell like dominoes until there was silence, leaving only three to stand in a field of steaming bodies. Stunned, they scrambled to turn their bikes around and retreat in the direction from which they had come.

Ben waited and watched for Jake to emerge from under the bridge, but there was no sign of him. After what Pete had said about the boy's energy level, he felt a rush of fear pass through him. He ran to the end of the bridge and down the embankment to see what was wrong, stopping cold at the sight.

Jake lay lifeless on the pavement in the middle of the right lane. Ben strained to detect any movement at all, as he scuttled over the fence and ran to him.

"Jake! Talk to me, buddy," he yelled at the lifeless boy.

Maire could hear Ben's voice rising up from the road below. She climbed over the center column of the truck and into the driver seat, throwing the idling engine into gear. The door slammed shut as the truck lurched forward. Pete bounced in his seat as she drove back down the embankment and stopped the truck.

Ben had moved Jake to the shoulder of the road and laid him in the sparse grass. He was bent over the boy. Maire cried out, "Is he...?" She and Pete were out of the truck and running to his side.

"I don't know."

Pete walked up and sniffed the unconscious young man. "I'm afraid he's..." He spoke in a halting somber voice as Maire began to wail and fell to her knees beside Jake.

"...Going to be just fine when he wakes up," the dog continued with a sly grin.

"You ass!" Maire slapped the dog on his hindquarters. "You let me believe he was dead!"

"Young lady, I believe it was you who did not allow me to finish what I was saying." The dog began to lick Jake's hand. "Wake up, my friend. There's no time to rest."

Immediately, Jake opened his eyes.

ELEVEN

Flying high above the Atlantic Ocean, the private jet traveled westward. In the pilot's seat was a hulking creature with a firm grip on the controls, and next to him, the purple-faced pilot stared straight ahead through the clouded eyes of death. He had protested loudly when the trio had boarded the luxurious small plane, but when Seraphine had given him the choice to either fly the plane or abandon it, he chose to stand his ground. His death had come quickly before he could change his mind, and Seraphine had quite enjoyed crushing the life from him.

In the passenger cabin, Betlamel was pouring a glass of wine for his mistress. He was having some trouble holding it steady due to a combination of turbulence and the substitute pilot's lack of skill. Neither he nor Frogoth had ever flown a plane before. Seraphine had transferred the knowledge from the mind of the dead man to Frogoth, but she had been in a hurry and there were gaps in the information. The poor beast was trying to sort it out as he went.

"Where is my wine?" Seraphine shouted over her shoulder as she looked out at the clouds.

Betlamel shoved the cork back into the bottle hastily and set it on the small counter. As he hurried to his mistress, there was a thud as the bottle fell to the floor and began rolling back and forth in the tiny alcove. He steadied himself against the seats as he worked his way down the aisle and handed her the glass.

"Is it always so rough, this way of flying? I'm certain the birds do not experience such ridiculous jouncing," she barked after taking a sip.

"I'm not sure, Mistress. I've never been in one of these machines before." He braced himself. Assuredly, whatever frustration she was feeling at the moment would be vented on him.

"Tell Frogoth to show improvement soon, or you will be claiming his seat and he will be flying on his own... out there!" She pointed out of the plane, tapping her well-manicured black fingernail against the window.

"Yes, Mistress. I will relay the message. Is there anything else I can do for you?"

He realized that it was entirely possible for Frogoth to be thrown from the plane. He wanted to warn his counterpart that he was at risk. Seraphine did not turn her face, but merely dismissed him with a wave of her arm. With a heavy sigh, he turned and headed toward the cockpit.

"Where and when are we landing?" Betlamel asked.

"We're going to a place called Shreveport. I have no idea of when we shall arrive. Why do you care?"

"Our mistress is not pleased with your flying skills, I'm afraid. She is threatening to eject you from the plane if you do not improve."

The creature took his eyes from the horizon and turned to face his friend. "And you would fly this machine? Ha! By the time she took my thoughts to show you how, there would not be much for you to glean. Tell her I will improve soon, or I will exit from the craft myself, willingly." He smiled wide and showed his large yellowed teeth. "And the both of you will perish in flames when it crashes."

Betlamel was not amused by his response. In fact, he found no humor in anything associated with this entire assignment. He and Frogoth had served others in the past, but never anyone so young or careless, and certainly none as powerful. Thus far, every moment they had spent with Seraphine had been a series of punishments and humiliation. The pair had worn weary of it all. Perhaps a flaming death in a plane crash would be merciful and save them both from their plight.

"Where is my food?" The woman bellowed from the rear of the plane.

Sighing, Betlamel began to move out of the cockpit. "Please don't cause this to end badly for us. I will go and feed her and take the punishment for both of us if it be necessary. You will owe me when the time comes, and I will be expecting my due." The huge man-like creature staggered back to the cabin before he could hear the response from his partner.

"You may expect it, but you should not count on it, my friend. I will sacrifice you to preserve myself if need be," he grumbled. "I plan to be here to see hell come to earth, and if that means sacrificing you to that end, so be it."

Shifting in his seat, Frogoth focused on the horizon and fiddled with the controls in an attempt to improve the steadiness of the aircraft.

TWELVE

Several hours later, making steady progress toward their destination, Ben was listening to country music on the radio as the sun was setting. Pete regularly checked the sides of the road and the mirror on his side for any possible threats. Jake and Maire were sound asleep in the back seat.

"Are we there yet?" Pete asked Ben, scratching his ear.

He laughed out loud. "Are you ten years old?"

"No, I am centuries old. I have seen much more of this world than you ever will in your short life, teacher."

Ben's laughter quickly died off. His voice became serious. "Yes, I'm sure that you have. Is that what makes you so short-tempered? Isn't age supposed to foster patience?"

"Patience is a virtue. As you might expect, my kind are lacking in virtuous behavior," the dog snapped back. "You should know this from your studies."

"My field of expertise is in ancient languages, Pete. I do not purport to know the culture of demons. Your kind has existed from the dawn of time and a lot of written texts speak of you as myth. My interest is in the language rather than the belief systems of people. Those things are a sidebar, so to speak."

"Believe this, my friend. With every passing moment, we are closing in on a major confrontation with the Invert. I am hoping we will be nearing the end of our mission before it comes. Jake will need to be rested and ready. He cannot continue using his powers to fight as he has been doing. You saw what the last conflict did to him. Facing another one too soon could definitely kill him."

"Yes, I know." Ben was growing tired of the current topic of conversation. "So, in your opinion, would it be better for us to go after the next scroll in daylight, or in darkness? Or does daylight make any difference to demons?"

"We will be safest while the sun is highest in the sky, but by no means is there ever a safe time of day. You witnessed this with the bikers, did you not?" Pete stared out the window at the darkening sky.

"True. In that case, let's look for a motel to get some rest for the night. We can eat, sleep, and leave in the morning. The crime rate in New Orleans is bad enough during daylight. I don't think we should push our luck at night."

"Push our luck with what?" Jake's voice came from the back.

"We've decided it will be better for us to roll into town in daylight, rather than at night. Pete thinks it will be safer. He says that we might be headed for a confrontation with the Invert." Ben was speaking to the young man's reflection in the rearview mirror.

"What makes you think the Invert is coming here, Pete?"

"There have been many attempts to kill you, all failures thus far. I believe they will come for you themselves."

"You speak of the Invert as if there is more than one." Ben checked the sign at the next exit for a motel.

"Because *they* are legion. The Invert possesses the spirits of many demons, absorbed into one during her Awareness. They are coming for you, Jake, because they are angry and aggravated by your penchant for survival. To them, your status is barely above a human mortal. They expected to be wearing your skin by now, not fighting for it."

Maire felt sick to her stomach. She wasn't sure how much more of this she could take. She wasn't married to the guy, but, well, she just loved him more than she had ever loved anyone else she had ever known. But, would that be enough to keep her going through it all, knowing that all of them could be killed at any moment? Of course, there was no other choice.

"I can do this." The words slipped easily out of her mouth.

"What can you do?" Jake turned to face her.

She had not realized that she had said it out loud and now she flushed with embarrassment. Instead of giving him a direct answer, she put her arms around him and pressed herself hard against him. She was prepared to stare death in the face for him. If it meant that she did not survive this, then so be it.

THIRTEEN

Betlamel was nursing some newly inflicted wounds in the attendants' compartment when he heard Frogoth announce their approach to the Shreveport runway. Quickly, he glanced around the corner to check on his mistress and found her asleep. *She had better be strapped in for the landing*, he thought, moving quickly to fasten her seatbelt. As he had hoped, she did not awaken.

Making certain to secure anything that could be tossed about during landing, he scurried back to the cockpit. Just as he stepped through the door, he could hear a loud muffled voice coming from the headset that lay on the floor between the pilots' seats.

"Is there a problem? Why do I hear the sound of someone shouting coming from that device?" Awkwardly, he bent to pick up the headset and put it to his ear. "They are saying there is a plane approaching... It is unauthorized for landing... It needs to turn sixty degrees west and assume a holding pattern. Are they talking to us?"

"I have no idea what that means. We are landing right now, right over there." He pointed a clawed hand at a runway that was currently unoccupied. "If you are afraid, strap yourself into that seat."

Betlamel looked over at the seat occupied by the dead pilot. Hastily, he unbuckled the belt holding the pilot and pulled the corpse up out of his seat before dropping him at the back of the cockpit where he landed with a thud in a pile of twisted arms and legs.

"Try not to kill us all, and maybe our mistress will allow you to keep all of your limbs intact when this is over."

"Hang on and shut up." Frogoth was holding the controls so tightly that it appeared they could snap off in his hands. The concrete runway was coming up quickly beneath them and the small plane began leveling off. "Here we go."

The wheels of the landing gear had nearly touched the ground when a large shadow appeared over the runway. With a roar, the 757 passed within several feet above them and the backwash from the engines slammed the smaller plane to the ground faster than expected. The downward pressure caused the private jet to bounce, and everything inside was jolted as the plane rose again. Oddly, the aircraft remained suspended, frozen in midair.

"What in the name of hell and everything evil is going on up there?" Seraphine's shrill voice came from just outside of the cockpit door. "Can't we do something as simple as land this damned plane?"

Frogoth turned to her with fire in his eyes. "Oh, you think it is so easy, you ungrateful piece of subhuman excrement!" It was then that he realized he had actually spoken the words aloud. He figured he was about to be vaporized anyway, and his eyes went wild as he finished his rant. "Go ahead, destroy me! Throw me to the huskers! I am done with this... this... this..." He stopped short, grasping at his throat as his voice was squeezed from it.

"I will not allow you to continue making a fool of yourself. Obviously, you intend to make a quick exit from this assignment, but that would be too easy for you." She let out a deep sigh. "No, you will land this plane, and then you will help me complete this mission. Then and only then will I decide what terrible torture awaits you. Now turn around and land this thing before I take my anger out on Betlamel."

The lumpy hulk of a pilot turned back to the controls as the plane began to move again. Even so, everything else around them continued to hang suspended like some creepy child's mobile, while the smaller jet landed and taxied down the runway, steering to avoid other aircraft that were frozen in place.

Reaching its destination, the other aircraft jerked back to life as though the incident never occurred, with the notable exception of two large passenger jets that had narrowly averted a tragic collision. By the time the sky over the Shreveport airport had returned to some semblance of normalcy, the evil trio had *borrowed* a stretch limo.

FOURTEEN

At about one o'clock in the afternoon, the black truck pulled into a parking space near the St. Louis cemetery in New Orleans. The black dog in the passenger seat was hanging out the window sniffing the air, checking for threats. Tinted windows kept anyone who might be curious from looking into the back seat and seeing the passengers who were working with the ancient book. Jake had just used the small golden knife to open a gash in the palm of his hand.

As the drops of blood spread through the pages, and the words began to appear, the answers that Jake sought were spelled out in ancient characters that only he and the professor could read. Ben wasn't as adept at the translation, but he often did well enough to get things started.

"Are we in the right place?" Maire was sitting next to Jake, looking at the book from her viewpoint. Unfortunately, she was unable to read what it said.

"It looks right according to the map, but I'm not convinced. This is a cemetery. Would someone hide a scroll in a place like this?"

"It makes perfect sense, Jake." Ben leaned on the center column. From where he was, he could see the red dot on the map that represented the scroll, and the other mark that he believed represented Jake. "We'll need to use caution though. We can't just walk right in and break into a crypt. We'll end up in jail."

"Do you see all the people walking around the place? I suggest that Jake uses the voice and asks them to leave. Fortunately, I do not yet sense any who are possessed." Pete's head was still hanging out the window.

From the back seat, Jake could barely hear him. "We need a plan. This isn't like Stone Mountain, a park that was vacated at night. Even if we were to return at night, this place is still out in the open... and there it goes."

He watched the map fading back into the blank page. "I'm getting so tired of feeding this book. It seems to require more blood all the time."

Lost in her thoughts, Maire decided to voice her opinions "What if we dressed as cemetery workers? No one would pay any attention to us. Everyone would assume that we had a reason to be working here." She had seen some city workers gathered around a sewer drain along their route. "Maybe we could get some of those safety vests that the workers wear."

"What workers?" Ben hadn't even noticed them. In New York, he was accustomed to seeing city workers everywhere he went.

"Why don't we just use the actual workers? It would seem more official, would it not?" Pete was recalling the mission at Stone Mountain. "The way we used the guards for cover at the rock mountain. We could have some workers stand near us while we retrieve the scroll. They won't remember what we were doing afterward, when we are gone."

"You're right. That's perfect. We'll have them stand around us while we crack open the crypt. Then we can grab the scroll and be long gone before they snap out of it." Jake hugged Maire. "Now all we have to do is get them from where they are working to this location. Ideas anyone?"

They sat in silence for a moment before he came up with the answer himself. "Ben, you go with Pete to find the crew we passed on the way here. Pete can use the voice and get them to come to the cemetery.

He can ride back with them in their truck and keep them controlled on the way."

"That almost sounds too easy, but I can't think of anything better. We can't sit around here too long, or we'll be facing another horde of crazy possessed people." Ben scratched his forehead and looked out the windshield. "Maire, how far away was that crew?"

"It was back on the main road near the bridge. There were three guys there with their city van."

"Okay, then. We'll go and get them. Make sure you're ready when we get back. You're going to have to cut yourself again, Jake. I know that sucks, but we need to know exactly which crypt we have to open. It's not like we can use trial and error, right?"

"Got it, Ben. We'll be ready. Make sure the men bring their tools. I don't think we'll be able to get into a crypt without them. I'm thinking sledgehammers and shovels. A road crew should have something like that."

Jake opened the door with the book in his hand. "We have to make this work. Good luck, see you when you get back." He climbed out of the truck.

Maire had not realized that she had been holding her breath until, at last, exhaled as she stepped out into the parking lot and stood next to Jake. "I can't believe what we've been through already, and we only have two scrolls." Her eyes followed the truck as it moved away, turned the corner and sped out of sight.

"Yeah, but retrieving this one seems simple enough. We find the crypt, bust it open, and grab the scroll. Then we're off to the next stop. Easy, greasy, done," Jake assured her. "Let's check the book again. I want to be ready when they get back. Like Ben said, we can't stay here long."

As he moved to find some place where they would not attract attention, he was distracted by the cawing of the crows circling overhead. "Something's wrong. I've never seen so many crows flying together."

He raised his head and shouted up at the birds. "What are you devils up to?" The voice came rolling from his lips, "Leave this place and fly out far above the ocean. Do not return to this place until tomorrow."

Jake's voice bent the sunlight like a mirage across hot pavement, and the crows were pushed along in its wake. There was no need to tell them twice. They immediately stopped circling, flew toward the river and followed it out to sea.

FIFTEEN

Ben sat with Pete in the van across the street from the three construction workers standing with their shovels, engrossed in conversation. Pete stared straight ahead, as Ben asked, "So you're just going to walk over there and order them to follow us to the cemetery?"

"Well, that's one way to do it, the most direct way, I suppose. Or, I could run around and bite at their heels, round them up like cattle."

Pete's deadpan stare always put a smile on Ben's face. "As much as I'd like to see that, I'd hate for you to catch a shovel to the side of your head." He rubbed his own head for effect. "What do you say we both go over there like I'm taking you for a walk, and then you can do your thing?"

"Sounds rather dull, however, it might be a rather good plan."

"Okay, so let's go." Ben climbed out of the truck and walked around to let the dog out. The pair paused to look for oncoming traffic and then continued across the street. As they approached the men, Ben spoke first. "Enjoying this beautiful day?"

"What?" The man with the biggest beer gut turned to his co-workers and laughed. "Where'd you get the poodle in the jacket?"

"It isn't a jacket. He's a service dog. Haven't you ever seen a service do…"

Pete cut Ben short. His voice was deep and smooth as he commanded, "You, in the red shirt. Take your shovel and smack the fool who made the poodle comment."

The man in the red shirt didn't blink as he swung his shovel and hit his partner square in the stomach.

The man barely had time to look surprised before doubling over.

Pete began barking orders. "All of you... gather your tools and put them in the van."

The men responded immediately and began picking up their shovels and the pile driver they had used to break up the concrete of the sidewalk where they were working.

"I don't understand how you direct your voice so that you control them. Why doesn't it affect me?" Ben would never get used to the way Pete and Jake could turn their power off and on at will.

"You want to crawl like a snake, teacher? I can include you if you wish. It would be rather humorous to have all four of you..."

"No, thank you very much. Jake is waiting for us. Aren't you riding with them?"

"I am afraid I don't have much choice. I don't have as much reach with my control as our friend does. I suppose I am forced to ride in their machine to guide them, as filthy as it looks."

Just then, the first man to reach the van threw open the side door and the truth of the dog's statement became even more apparent. Several tools and tangled extension cords fell out onto the curb.

Ben laughed, "Well, enjoy that ride, Petey-boy. I'll get the truck. Just have them follow me to the cemetery." He ran back across the street while Pete loaded his new crew of followers into their van.

"Do any of you own a bar of soap? You smell ripe as the dead. I will sit in the front. Open the door for me."

The one nearest the door opened it and Pete jumped in.

"Okay, now shut the door and get in the back."

The man closed the door and the three of them forced themselves into the small space in front of the tools that covered the floor, closing the door of the van behind them. Pete turned looked at them in disbelief. Not one of them attempted to get into the driver's seat.

"Excuse me, mindless ones. Which one of you drove the van to this location?"

Two of them pointed at one who raised his hand.

"Please get into the driver's seat and start driving before I bite you."

The one who had raised his hand scrambled between the seats and sat behind the wheel.

"Very well then, follow the black truck wherever it goes, and don't lose sight of it."

***

Maire stood watch while Jake once again sliced open the palm of his hand and allowed his blood to flow onto the page of the book.

"I don't see anybody. Is the map visible yet?"

"Yeah, let's go."

He held the open book in his hand and started walking down the path between the crypts that housed the remains of the dead.

"We're getting closer, the spot is right ahead." Continuing about ten more steps, he came to a stop. "Here it is."

The small concrete structure was nearly eight feet high and was constructed from partially exposed red brick. A short iron fence surrounding the front of it was connected by a somewhat useless gate. Maire tried it and found it allowed easy access.

"This can't be right." Jake turned the book around. "Just as we stopped here, another dot appeared on the map. Wait, something is happening." He gazed at the page as words began to appear next to the map in the margin.

"That book is so strange, like it's alive or something." Maire watched as the words wrote themselves with an invisible hand. "What does it say?"

"Give me a minute. I need to figure it out. It's like a riddle or something."

"Maybe I can help. Read it out loud to me."

"I don't know, Maire. It's confusing enough for me. I don't think you can…" Then he saw the look on her face. It spoke of slashing fingernails and grinding teeth. Right away, he realized he should not have dismissed her outright like that. He decided he had better read the words out loud or there might be trouble.

"Okay, here goes: *The distance by ten, the front to the chamber, the breath is the weakness, and held in wet darkness. To gain what you seek, you will stroke to the end, and in that last moment your will you must bend.*"

He looked blankly at the page. "So what the hell does that mean?"

"I think it means the scroll is going to be harder to get than simply opening up the crypt and grabbing it."

She walked to the side of the crypt and looked at what lay beyond it. She wasn't sure exactly what it meant, but she began to have a strange, tingling sensation. When everything around them became normal again, the young couple was left standing and staring quizzically at one another. A moment or so later, the sound of a barking dog broke the silence.

Maire whispered, "I think they're back, I recognize that voice."

Jake whistled and hollered, "Over here!" He hoped they had heard him. He did not want to have to call out to them again.

Ben turned the corner and started walking their way with three men in fluorescent green vests following him. They were carrying their tools, and Pete was close behind them. As they drew closer, Jake could see shovels, a pry bar and a sledgehammer in the hands of the city workers.

"Did you have any trouble?" Jake asked as the crew reached them.

"No trouble, but these guys obviously embrace the natural life. I don't think any one of them has bathed in the last decade," Pete commented, sardonic as usual. "I felt like I was trapped in a closed container of filthy armpits."

Ben laughed. "I don't know why they carry so many tools in their truck. They didn't seem to be using any of them when we pulled up. From what I saw, they just stand around and talk."

Maire was surprised that her friends were talking about the workers that way while the butts of their jokes stood expressionless next to them, waiting for their orders. Likely, these men would have strongly objected to the derisive remarks under normal circumstances. Instead, they stared straight ahead and said nothing.

"Let's get to it then," Jake insisted. He shuffled his feet, eager to complete the mission and get out of New Orleans in one piece. "If they're going to look as though they're official, then they need to get to work. They should behave just as they do on the street."

"Release them, Pete," he added. "I'll take it from here. I'll need you to be alert for any interference from visitors, or worse yet, some possessed crazies."

"Believe me, I'm more than glad to be finished with these men. Absolutely no challenge in those thick skulls." He yelped once, and it was as though the puppet strings were cut. The men looked at each other, their eyes filled with confusion.

"Hold onto your tools and face the crypt." Jake's voice wrapped around them and they straightened, turning as one toward the small brick structure. "You, with the beard, pick up the sledgehammer and open up that crypt, and you two," he said to the others, "act natural. Lean on your shovels and talk about sports or something."

"Sports!" Ben blurted out. "You think these guys talk about sports? I'm guessing they talk about some things that are a little more entertaining than that if you know what I mean."

The man was pounding on the old bricks with the sledge, smashing at the face of the crypt repeatedly.

"What do you mean?" Maire asked over the noise. "What do you think they would talk about?"

She had no clue about men such as these and was about to get an answer that she wouldn't like when Jake interrupted, "It doesn't matter. The crypt is nearly opened. Let's try to get a look."

They stepped forward in time to see the man pulling out the last few bricks. Jake squinted, trying to get a look. "The sun is so bright out here that it makes it seem even more dark in there. We need a flashlight. I'm not going to stick my arm in there when I can't see a thing. I know there are snakes around here, but there might be gators, too."

Ben turned and ran for the truck, calling back over his shoulder, "I'm on it."

"You honestly think there could be a gator in there? Seems like it was sealed up pretty good." Maire tried to see around Jake and get a look into the black interior of the crypt.

"I don't know, but Pete warned me that if I ever lose an arm or a leg, it won't grow back. Apparently, I can heal wounds but nothing as catastrophic as loosing a limb. That's why I'm not taking any chances."

Jake tried shielding his eyes from the blinding sunlight, but he still couldn't see. Right now, the only thing he knew for sure was that he must be as prepared as possible for what lay ahead.

Sixteen

The black limousine was parked at a crowded rest area south of Shreveport. Around the grassy park, people stood as still as stone statues. Children in the small playground area were suspended in time, frozen in place as they had been climbing, swinging and sliding before the odd trio arrived.

In the center of the park, the stillness was broken. A young woman was speaking with a large crow that had perched itself on one of the concrete picnic tables. The blank stares all around them revealed that no one was aware of the strange happenings in their midst.

"So tell me, bird, where can I find the one I am seeking?" Arms crossed, she stood waiting for the response.

"He and his band of friends are at the old cemetery in New Orleans. They arrived there only a short time ago, and it appears they are searching for something."

The old crow turned and squawked at another who had landed in a nearby tree. Once he got a response, he added, "They are several hours from here using your current mode of travel. If you are not able to fly, you should leave now or you may miss them."

"I expect you will have guides in the sky between here and there?" She looked up at the blue sky. "You must take us to them immediately."

"Yes, Mistress. My brethren and I will form a trail in the sky that you will be able to follow. We will guide you straight to them."

"Quickly then, and be attentive. We will follow your lead." She turned and strutted toward the car as her hulking bodyguards followed close behind. Within minutes, they were on the highway headed to the Mississippi Delta, a black winged line in the sky leading the way.

SEVENTEEN

Jake held the beam of the flashlight steady through the opening of the crypt to light up the darkness. "It's flooded. I can't see anything but water."

"What did the book tell you about this place? Did you check it?" Soaked with sweat, Ben was still catching his breath after running to the truck and back.

"There were two dots on the map. One indicated this exact location, right here where we're standing. The other one, presumably the location of the scroll, was located over that way." He pointed toward a large old tree. "There was a riddle, too, but I wasn't sure what it meant."

"Jake, I think I know what it means, now that we have the crypt opened up," Maire offered. She had been standing guard, watching for anyone who might approach, while Pete continued his watch in the opposite direction.

Ben waited for her to complete her thought, but her silence forced him to prod her, "And?"

"Well, I think there is a tunnel down there, and the scroll should be at the end of it. The riddle mentioned something about breath, and then stroking, and then bending. It looks like this goes back about twenty feet on the map. Didn't the riddle start with 'the distance by ten'? That would be two feet."

As though a light had turned on in Jake's head, his expression changed and he started to take off his shirt.

"What are you doing?" Ben asked as Jake handed him his shirt.

"I'm going to go in there and get that scroll." He was unbuttoning his pants.

"Leave your clothes on, Jake. We might have to make a quick getaway and, seriously, you don't want to get caught with your pants down. I think we should check it out before you go in there. Maybe we can find out what's in the water. Tell one of the workers to stick his arm in and see what's there. It's possible that there's not even a tunnel anymore. It might have collapsed when that hurricane flooded everything here," Ben insisted. He handed the shirt back to Jake and pushed one of the workers toward the crypt.

"Will that make you feel better about it?" Jake was somewhat concerned. He did not like subjecting the compliant man to any unnecessary risk.

"Yes, please. Tell him to use his hand and feel around for what's down there."

"Okay, you heard him. Dig down in there and pull out anything you find."

Jake stood back as the man dropped to his knees and went straight to work. In seconds, the first of the bones came up. A pile began to form as various sections of human remains were removed including a jawless skull. He thrust his arm into the water until it nearly covered his shoulder and pulled fistfuls of small bones from the depths of darkness. Finally, when his hand began to come up empty, he pulled his arm out and got to his feet. Turning glassy-eyed toward his puppet master, he stepped back out of the way.

"I'm going in." Jake had removed his shoes and socks and leaned into the crypt. He pulled back out and announced, "I'm going to have to go in at an angle, almost lying down. It looks like it could be tight. Be ready to pull me out when I get back."

He turned to look for the dog, who was still standing watch. "Hey, Pete! I need you over here."

The dog's ears were perked up as he twisted his head around to see what was going on. He stood up and trotted over to the group. "Yes? You have a plan?"

"I'm going in after the scroll. Can I count on you to keep the workers in line until I get back?"

"Of course, my friend. Don't worry. You just stay safe in there."

With that, Jake got down on his hands and knees, "Give me the flashlight, Ben. I hope it's waterproof," he said as he took the light from his friend. Sucking in a large breath of air, he slid headfirst into the crypt and disappeared into the black water.

EIGHTEEN

The tunnel was not much wider than his body, and Jake was pushing his way through the murky water. He moved along, stirring up the muck from years of floods and decomposing bodies, whose skeletal remains were scattered on the bottom of the stone crawlway. He hadn't calculated how difficult it was going to be to hold his breath for so long, and his lungs were beginning to burn. Apprehensive about what would await him at the end of this hellish swim, Jake remained focused on getting to the end of it.

At last, he reached the roots of the tree that had grown down into the end of the tunnel. Fumbling with the flashlight, he turned it toward the thick growth. There appeared to be a large pocket of air above him, and he moved rapidly forward and up to catch his breath. Overwhelmed by the musty smell, he gagged on the stench he was forced to inhale with his first breath. His airway was coated with the smell of death.

The walls of the small chamber were covered by veils of tiny roots that hung like curtains and obscured the prize that he had come to retrieve. Holding the light in one hand, he used the other to tear at the obstruction, pulling it apart until finally he could see what appeared to be the end of a scroll in the highest possible spot above the waterline. Reaching out to grab hold of it, he found it tightly wedged between the roots.

Shifting his body, he put his feet against the short stone wall above the crawl space and braced himself so he could pull harder. He laid the flashlight on a dirt ledge and grabbed the scroll with both hands, pulling with every ounce of strength he had.

Gradually, the scroll came loose, and the stone wall collapsed beneath his feet along with the ledge where he had placed the light. All of it fell beneath him, sealing off his path of return. He had liberated the scroll, but now he was imprisoned in the foul dark hole that remained. He would soon run out of air if he could not find a way out.

***

Outside the crypt, Maire was pacing. "He's been in there way too long. Something has happened, I'm sure of it! We need to help him."

"I don't know if it's been too long or not. I'm not sure what to do." Ben had been trying to maintain his composure for her until now. He began wringing his hands.

Pete remained silent. He had been confident that his friend would be successful. After all, the boy had done amazing things since coming into his awareness. Now, even he was beginning to think that his friend was in trouble. He needed to do something.

"You, grab your shovels and get to that tree," he barked at the workers. Running around the crypt, he headed to the tree as he spoke. He realized that what he was about to do was likely a futile attempt to rescue Jake.

"Get over here and start digging as fast as you can," he growled at the men who instantly began digging like crazed machines around the base of the trunk. *Thunk. Thunk.* Each time the shovels were thrust into the ground, they hit a root. Although they continued to try, the men could only penetrate a few inches into the ground before hitting a solid wooden barrier.

Maire and Ben abandoned the crypt and ran to catch up to others, taking a position well away from the swinging shovels. Maire clutched Jake's shoes and socks to her chest. For now, all she could do was watch.

"There's got to be something I can do to…" Ben was holding the heavy pry bar, but he was not one for using heavy tools.

"Give me a minute, professor." Pete turned to bark at the men, "Keep trying until you are told to stop."

***

Down below, Jake was very glad to be in an open air space despite the fact that his legs were beginning to cramp. Now that the tunnel had collapsed and his legs were partially covered in the dirt, there was little room to move around. His mind was rushing, running through any number of strategies. Choking on the stale musty air, he could hear the faint thumping sounds coming from above. He felt a twinge of fear as he wondered how long it would be before he had used up all of the oxygen.

"I'm down here!"

He listened for some acknowledgement that he had been heard. There was no other sound but the continued thumping from above. How far below the surface he was situated, he had no way to know. Roots from a tree this old would have to run deep. Even if his friends could dig through the ground above, would they be able to reach him in time? Did they even know where he was? What if they were digging in the wrong place? Any further collapse could bury him alive.

"Can you hear me? I'm down here!"

He forced the words out with more volume this time. Suddenly, he felt the ground shaking around him. Dirt that had been lodged in the roots above him now loosened and dropped down in clumps, covering him to his waist. Another attempt could bury him in the suffocating mud. Still, there was no sign that anyone had heard him.

***

"Did you feel that?" Maire knelt down and touched the ground. "Was that an earthquake?"

"It is not unusual to have minor earthquakes anywhere." Ben looked up. "Look at the tree, the branches are shaking but there's no wind from any direction."

"He's moving it from below." Pete was sniffing at the roots that had been exposed by the workers. "I don't know how, but Jake did this. Whatever he did, he needs to do it again."

The dog sat down where he was, and raised his head toward the sky. "Get ready to move out of the way. Something amazing is about to happen." He waited for the ground to shake again.

***

Considering how the ground had shaken the last time he called out, Jake wondered what would happen if he tried it again, this time using the hypnotic voice. There was only one way to find out. He drew in as much stale air as he could manage without gagging and mentally focused on moving the earth. With closed eyes, he began to shout using *the voice*.

***

"Stand back and cover your ears." Pete barely had time to bark out the words before the rumbling began again. From beneath them came a wailing sound unlike any they had ever heard before, and the dog was right to warn them. Even with their ears covered, it was painful to hear. Pete began to howl along.

The ground was quaking, as the noise grew louder, and the gravestones nearby began cracking and crumbling into piles of rough gravel. The tree shook violently and small branches fell all around the base of the tree. The large roots were pulling out of the ground at the feet of the group, and they quickly stepped back out of the way. It was as though a large hand was reaching down from the sky and yanking the tree, roots and all, from the ground. Without warning, it flew high into the air above them. Maire screamed as she backpedaled in retreat.

As suddenly as it had gone up, the whole tree crashed to the ground just yards from where it had stood. The wailing sound faded, and Pete's howl was becoming more muted. While everyone's attention was distracted by the great broken tree lying in the open courtyard of the cemetery, a muddy arm shot up out of the ground.

Maire let out an audible gasp as she turned to find Jake crawling out of the hole with the scroll tucked under his arm. She stood gaping, in shock, as he wiped the dirt from his face and blinked in the bright sunlight. Finally, she reached out for him, closing the distance between them until she could touch his face and wipe away some of the mud caked on his cheek.

"Good to see you, Jake," Ben greeted him calmly, as though pushing a tree over and climbing out from under it were an everyday occurrence. "We best get moving." He nodded toward the group of people who were closing in to see what had caused the seismic event.

One glance at the growing crowd and Jake gave direction to the three workers who had been watching his every move. "You guys stay here and explain to the people that they need to stand back. Do whatever it takes to keep them away until we are gone." Considering how they might interpret what he had said, he quickly added, "but don't hurt anyone!" Clutching the scroll a little more tightly, he led his friends back to the truck, clumps of mud dropping from his body as he jogged along.

"We need to get you cleaned up before we leave town," Maire noted. "How are we going to accomplish that without a hotel room?"

"We can look for a truck stop along the highway," Ben suggested, as they reached the vehicle. Maire got in first and covered the seat with a towel that had been tucked away in the back before Jake climbed in.

"We should check the book for our next destination before we leave, don't you think?" Pete hopped into the front passenger seat. "How did you know to use the voice, Jake? I never knew it was possible to move objects with it, especially something as large and secure as a tree."

"So why did you howl along, if you didn't know?" the muddy young man asked.

"It seemed like the thing to do at the time, and it turns out, it was the right thing. By the way, I'm not sure you are aware, but you smell really bad." Pete moved to get as far away from the stench as possible.

NINETEEN

Jake studied the map in the book while the others leaned in to see for themselves. A large black dot was moving slowly toward a smaller red one. Jake scratched his head in silence and tiny chunks of dirt fell to his shoulders like dandruff.

"This can't be right," he complained. Pete shifted in the front seat to get a better view. "That map definitely is not Paris, but the mark there is the Invert, and I believe that the red dot is us. I hope I'm wrong because that would mean that the Invert is getting closer to us."

"Drive, Ben. Go now." Jake was more than a little nervous about this discovery. He certainly hadn't expected to meet his nemesis so early in his quest.

"Where am I going? What's the next stop?" Ben asked as he pulled into traffic. "I can't just drive around. I need some direction."

The red dot on the map moved slightly closer to the black one.

"We need to go the other way!" Maire shouted at Ben. "Turn around, and hurry!"

After checking his mirrors, Ben turned the wheel and pulled a wide U-turn in the middle of the street. The truck's tires squealed against the pavement, as they sped off in the other direction. Now the map showed the red dot easily gaining distance from the black dot.

"The Invert doesn't seem to be moving. Maybe they're stuck in traffic. There should be another map here showing where we can find the next scroll." Jake flipped the page and there it was.

***

Seraphine was screaming from the back seat of the limo as the traffic ahead of them ground to a complete stop. "Get out and see what is keeping us from moving!"

Betlamel reluctantly opened the door and stepped out onto the pavement. From where he stood, he could see miles of cars stretching out ahead of them, but there was no sign of what was preventing their progress. He looked to the sky and saw that the crows were in a holding pattern, circling above. Putting his hands around his mouth, he yelled up to them, "Send your leader down here immediately."

In a moment, a large crow was standing on the pavement before him. "Yes, you summoned me? How can I be of service to you?" The crow shifted nervously on its feet.

"What is stopping this line of vehicles? My mistress wishes to know why we're not moving?"

"There was a terrible accident. It appears that people were killed, and the road is blocked."

"Can we go around it?"

"Unless you drive on the other side of the road, against the traffic, you will not be able to go around it. I do not advise that course of action. It would not go well for you, I'm afraid."

Tilting his head, the bird continued, "I'm afraid that is not the only bad news. We have not heard from our friends in the city for some time. We will continue to lead you to the location where those you pursue were last seen, but there is no way to be certain that they will be there when we arrive."

Betlamel did not hide the expression of shock on his face. There was no way he could tell his mistress what he had just heard, so he ordered the crow to wait while he pulled Frogoth from the car.

"I am having trouble understanding this bird. You try listening to it, so you can inform the mistress."

Frogoth looked annoyed as he walked toward the crow. "What is it? What are you trying to say?"

The crow repeated its report on the delay and the loss of communication with the crows in the city.

Frogoth turned to his partner and hissed, "Exactly what about that could you not understand? The bird spoke perfectly."

"I don't know, maybe it was the southern accent." Betlamel tried to keep from smirking. "So what did the bird say?"

"I will not waste my breath by repeating it twice." He stomped toward the driver side of the car, climbing in to relay the message he had been given.

The shriek from the limousine emitted a violent sound wave, which nearly threw Betlamel off his feet. Around them, the cars lifted ever so slightly off the pavement. With a thud, they all dropped back to earth and rocked on their springs as the wave passed. The brutish bodyguard steadied himself as he caught sight of the terrified expressions of the people around him. Men, women, and children were fighting the urge to evacuate their vehicles and run.

Suddenly, dozens of dead crows began to rain down from the sky…

***

"Mexico? I've never been to Mexico, have you?" Jake was cutting his hand again as he spoke. Once again, the book had to be fed in order to reveal additional details about their next destination.

"I was in Cancun once for a convention. We toured Chichen Itza and discussed the ancient Mayans and the carvings on the stones around the pyramids there." Ben watched in the rearview mirror as the young man squeezed blood from the palm of his hand onto the page of the book. "No matter how many times you do that, it still makes me wince."

"I've been to Mexico, back in the wild days. I can tell you, dogs do not have the same standing there as they do here. Most of them were roaming the streets instead of living pampered in a home with humans." Pete's face took on the sentimental glow of one fondly reminiscing on an earlier time of his life. He added, "There were many dog fights. For gambling purposes, of course. I had to kill a lot of dogs before I could finally leave that place."

"Why couldn't you use the voice on them?" Maire had a hard time believing that the dog would have subjected himself to that. "You could have just said a few words and walked out."

"I suppose so. I guess there was something about the whole thing that intrigued me. That kind of raw violent existence gave me a sense of mortality that I couldn't have experienced otherwise. Those dogs were warriors. They fought bravely for their masters and their own lives. Ultimately, most of them died in battle or, when gravely injured, at the hands of their human. Somehow, it gave me a greater sense of purpose for a time."

"That's so... I don't know how to put it... tragic, or... well, I don't know what to say." Maire reached out and stroked the dog's head, forgetting for the moment that he did not appreciate such expressions of affection. She was surprised when he leaned into the attention and closed his eyes allowing her continue. "How did you escape that place after all that?"

"One day, I was controlling a German shepherd host, you know, from inside him. I was fighting a large bulldog they called 'El Diablo Grande' or the Great Devil. After the first round, I had sustained a huge gash on my back and was bleeding badly. I spotted a beautiful woman in the crowd holding one of the smallest dogs I had ever seen. She held onto that dog as though it was her child, and I wondered what that kind of life would be like. So, instead of trying to win the fight, I allowed the other dog to kill my host. As the last breath came from the German shepherd's body, I leapt into the small dog and displaced it."

"What happened to the spirit of the small dog?" Jake was quite intent on listening to Pete's story and did not notice that the pages of the book were beginning to fade away again.

"It was, as I said, displaced. When I enter a body, the spirit stays with the body until I leave it. If the host dies, its spirit goes wherever it would have gone if it had died a natural death. If I leave the body before the host dies, then the spirit can return and resume its life."

"So the spirit of the dog you are in right now is here with us?" Ben had been paying closer attention to Pete's story than he was to the road.

"How else would I be able to remember anything the dog did before I moved in? I can hear its thoughts sometimes when everything is quiet."

"What does it think about?" Maire had never heard of such things. There were a lot of questions going through her mind.

"Mostly food, sex, elimination. However, occasionally it stops to wonder where it is or where its master is. Those kinds of thoughts are not unique to this species of animal. They are all very much alike and loyal to those who care for them."

"Oh, that's so sad." Maire wiped the wetness from her eye.

"Crap!" Jake was looking down at the book. "Great story, Pete. Now I have to cut myself again. What do you say we figure out exactly where we have to go before the next show starts?"

His friends looked at him with genuine concern. It was clear they thought that he had lost some humanity in the course of this ordeal, but Pete understood completely. The mission must come before anything else. The fate of *all* humanity was riding on the success of this one young man, and it was a burden greater than any of them could fully comprehend.

TWENTY

"This is totally unacceptable!" Seraphine pounded her fist against the seat as she looked around. "We must get moving. Every moment wasted in this forsaken wasteland allows them more time to escape."

Betlamel had become deft at shifting blame to anyone but himself. With the information he had gleaned from the crow, he offered a suggestion. "The crow suggested that we could cross the median to the other side and use that roadway to reach our destination. Although, he did claim it could be dangerous to do so."

He was secretly pleased. He was about to prove wrong every accusation his mistress had ever made about his stupidity. "We could do as he suggested..." he began, pausing for effect, "...and you could move the vehicles out of the way, just as you stopped the planes at the airport. You could easily push them out of the way and clear a path for us." He allowed himself a slow intake of air. "We may have to go with more care, but it is possible that we could reach them before they have slipped from our grasp."

Seraphine gazed out the window as he spoke. She met his suggestion with a long stretch of silence before responding, "Frogoth, can you get to the other side without getting us mired in the tall grass?"

"Yes, Mistress, I..."

"Imbecile! What are you waiting for? Let's get going. I will push the traffic out of the way, but it will be up to you not to run into anything after I clear the road."

She reached for a newspaper that lay on the floor as she barked her commands. Frogoth turned the wheel of the limo and hit the gas. The ground beneath them provided a bumpy ride and a few close calls with some hidden patches of mud. A few moments later, they emerged onto the opposite side of the highway.

The oncoming traffic was light at first, and the cars flashed their lights and blew their horns as they veered off, missing the black limo coming toward them. When Seraphine finally looked up from her paper and focused her attention on what was happening in front of them, it was as though an invisible snowplow began clearing the way ahead of their car.

Frogoth increased his speed as he became better at navigating through the swerving vehicles. The limo sped along while cars, trucks, and anything else in their way slid to either side of the road. Vehicles were flipping and rolling away in front of them as they continued to pick up speed. The wake of devastation behind them was growing by the second.

It wasn't long before the highway patrol was dispatched in their direction, and pursued them by car, helicopter and tow truck. Frogoth was gripping the steering wheel so tightly that his hands began to turn a bright shade of purple. Although he wore an expression of terror, it was not because of the law enforcement personnel in pursuit of them. He knew his mistress could handle them. What terrified him was the growing multitude of near misses, and though it was freaking him out, he dared not slow down. He had experienced enough punishment for today.

Seraphine looked up through the sunroof at the helicopter that was pacing them as it hovered above. Her annoyance was building. If they had any idea who they were dealing with, they would surely leave her alone. She had been quietly raging at all the setbacks they had already encountered along the way. It was time to unleash her vengeance on something greater than a small flock of crows.

"Betlamel, please observe. Today you shall bear witness as to why it is unwise to cross me. You will see that you are lucky to be alive after your outburst aboard the aircraft."

The brawny servant turned his head to watch as Seraphine raised her hand toward the helicopter. Closing her fingers as though gripping an unseen controller, she twisted her arm to the left and the helicopter moved in the same direction. Pleased, she jerked her arm to the right and swung her fist toward the floor. Betlamel could clearly see the expression of horror on the face of the pilot as the chopper slammed to the ground in a fiery explosion.

What the horrified hulk could not see was the look on Frogoth's face. While Seraphine's focus had shifted from the oncoming traffic to the helicopter, she was no longer shielding the limo from the vehicles coming toward them. The instant the chopper exploded, Frogoth was distracted enough to look away just as the tractor-trailer headed straight for them. At such a high rate of speed, the limo was unable to avoid it.

It was as though the collision had happened in slow motion, the front of the large car crushed by the large truck as it moved forward. Betlamel and Frogoth had been thrown into the windshield when the vehicle came to abrupt halt. The safety glass, smeared with their blood as it shattered, had not given way. The two unfortunate servants had been helplessly trapped between the seat and the dashboard barely an instant before the crushing moment of impact that ended their existence.

The front of the truck pushed up as it rolled over them, and the limo collapsed downward into the pavement as though flattened by a scrap yard crusher. The trailer broke loose and tumbled into the grass median that separated the lanes of the highway. Finally, the entire mass of twisted wreckage slid to a stop with the full weight of the truck resting atop the car.

Traffic behind them piled up as vehicles ground to a stop and frantic drivers rushed to the scene to render aid, checking to see if anyone could be saved. It seemed doubtful to anyone that there could be any survivors inside the limo. The driver inside the cab of the truck was found slumped over the wheel. As rescuers pulled the unconscious man out of the smoldering wreckage, the engine began to smoke, then exploded into flames.

TWENTY-ONE

"Did you see that? The black dot faded and disappeared all of a sudden. What do you think it means?" Jake was still rubbing his hand where it had just finished healing from the last time it was cut.

Pete hopped into the back seat to check out the page at close range. "This is important, very important. It could mean that the Invert has been eliminated, but then, how could it have happened?"

Ben turned on the radio and switched it to AM, listening for a news report. After skipping through many channels, he finally found something.

"...an update on the accidents with fatalities that have occurred on Highway 10. Earlier, we reported that there was a two-car collision as you head into New Orleans. This has now been cleared and traffic has begun to move again. Still smoldering in the outbound lane, however, is a pile-up awaiting investigation involving a wrong-way driver in a limousine and a tractor-trailer. It is undetermined how a highway patrol helicopter came to be involved, as well as several other vehicles. We'll have further details at..."

"Whoa! You could be right, Pete." Ben switched the radio off. "I'm guessing that was the end of the Invert since the mark has disappeared at the same time as that accident. I'm thinking we could be out of danger. Perhaps we should celebrate?"

Jake remained silent. It was difficult to believe that the threat to all mankind had just perished in a highway accident. He had a nagging feeling that something was not right, no matter what the disappearing mark in the book seemed to indicate.

Ben continued, "I think we should get a hotel room, clean ourselves up and celebrate with a nice dinner. We can leave in the morning for Mexico."

"You're probably right. We've been running for days now, and I can see how tired everyone is." Jake looked around at their faces. "However, I think it's too soon to celebrate. I don't feel right about this."

"Well, you definitely need to clean up, but I'd be happy if we head to the location of the next scroll right away. The sooner we get this town behind us, the less trouble we'll face. It is best to stay ahead of our enemies." Pete stopped as the spirit of the dog managed to insert one random word into his thoughts. "Steak."

Jake laughed, "That's the dog in you coming out."

"I don't know where that came from." Pete looked embarrassed as though he had just burped.

"Here's a place!" Maire had been searching the web on her new phone. "The Renaissance Hotel looks awesome. They have a 5-star restaurant, so we won't have to go out."

Pete looked at Jake, Jake looked at Ben, and all three of them said at the same time, "Sounds good!"

***

Jake felt so much better. He was showered and dressed in clean clothes. As he came out of the bathroom, the group was discussing the options for dining.

"I think I'm going to stay in the room and order room service for Pete and me." Jake perused the room service menu and pointed to the filet as he showed it to Pete.

"As if I can read? Is it steak?" Pete growled

"Better than steak, buddy. This is the good stuff."

Maire glared at Jake until finally voicing her opinion. "Is this how it's going to be now? Just Ben and me? I thought maybe, just maybe, we could spend some time together. I mean, since we're not off somewhere trying to get ourselves killed for some scroll."

"Sorry, Maire, but it does make sense," Ben agreed with Jake, which irritated Maire even more. "You haven't thought about how it would be if some demon-possessed waiter stuck a knife in Jake's neck while we're eating. Don't you think we should do whatever we can to keep him away from public exposure until this thing is over?"

"Well, what if we don't make it to the end? All this fear and sacrifice will be for nothing." Her tears began to well up as she imagined running for the exit.

Jake moved closer to her and put his arm around her. "I understand, Maire, really I do. It would be terrible if that happens, but this... this quest is my destiny, and I can't do anything to change it. You must know that. When things are back to normal, our relationship is and always will be the most important thing to me. I really do love you." He squeezed her and kissed the top of her head.

His profession of love had caught her off guard. "And I love you, too." Maire wiped the tears from her eyes once more. "Okay, you're right about the plan. You and Pete will probably get better service up here anyway. Ben and I will go down to the restaurant. I just want to pretend that life *is* back to normal, if only for an hour or so."

She went into the bathroom to freshen her makeup and called out to the others, "This must be what it's like to be a rock star. Stay in a beautiful place and never leave the room for fear of being torn apart by the fans. That's not much of a life."

"So... we better get going before it gets too crowded." Ben was smiling. "These upper crust folks eat late, and they'll be heading down there soon."

"Yeah, and don't let any of my *fans* follow you back up here, okay?" Jake teased.

Maire came from the bathroom and kissed him. "Order something good. You can bet we're going to. Let's go, Ben."

The pair closed the door, and Jake picked up the phone. Dialing the number for room service, he paused for someone to pick up and then read from the menu. "Yeah, I'll have the filet with bacon mashed potatoes, a shrimp cocktail, the caviar plate and a cheeseburger with everything. Oh, and fries smothered in chili, if you have it."

"What is a caviar plate, and you ordered a drink made with shrimp?" Pete tilted his head in confusion.

***

Maire and Ben ordered and sipped at their ice water while waiting for the appetizer. It was time to figure out the next leg of their journey, and Maire was scrolling through the screens on her phone.

"I don't think we should fly commercial. There are some charter jets listed for the airport. We should call about hiring one."

"I certainly do like the way you think," Ben responded. "We could have drinks served on board and indulge ourselves in luxury." He couldn't help it. He was happy just thinking about it, until the smile faded from his face. "Damn! I just remembered.

I don't have my passport with me. We left in such a hurry that I didn't think to bring it!"

"Passport? I don't have one either. Jake has his. I remember seeing it in his bag."

"We'll be asked to show them before we get on the plane, and again when we arrive. We're screwed."

The mood at the table was dampened. Not only were they going to be flying hundreds of miles away for the next scroll, now there was the issue of the missing legal documents. They sat in silence while the server brought their food and set the plates in front of them. Maire poked around her plate with her fork. Glancing up, she found Ben grinning again.

"The *voice*," he told her. "Jake, or even Pete, can use the voice whenever we need to talk to authorities. We don't have a problem at all. They can make us invisible if need be. Let's eat!"

TWENTY-TWO

Around 3:30 the next afternoon, the three friends and their service dog were greeted by a cheerful flight attendant at the door of the privately owned plane. She showed them around the luxurious interior and helped them stow their gear. Noticing the swords sticking out of one of the duffle bags, she raised her eyebrows but did not comment. She quietly stowed the bag in a compartment and checked to make sure her guests were aware of the safety features on board the aircraft.

"This is really nice, Maire. I'm glad you thought of it. Hey, Pete, is that seat good enough for you?" Jake laughed. Pete was turning in circles on one of the cushioned bench seats until at last he lay down.

"Yes, very good, much better than the seat in the truck and a lot softer." He rested his head on the cushion and watched as the flight attendant made last minute adjustments to her workstation.

"According to our flight plan, we will arrive in Cancun at approximately 5:30 p.m. local time. Please keep your seatbelts fastened during takeoff, and if there is anything at all you need during the flight, do not hesitate to ask." She sat in her seat and fastened her seatbelt before adding, "We'll be departing momentarily."

Pete growled at Jake, and the attendant looked startled. If she had been able to understand, she would have heard him ask if there was anything good on the menu. A few minutes later, the jet taxied down the runway and lifted gently into the air. All of the passengers were comfortable and relaxed as the plane banked and headed south to Mexico.

***

Later that same afternoon, Paul Tamlin was working late. As an investigator for the Department of Transportation, he had been dispatched to the wrecking yard to check out a limousine that had been crushed in a fatal accident. It had literally been flattened under the weight of a large tractor-trailer and partially melted in the resulting fire. It seemed obvious that no one could have survived such a thing, and he spoke into a pocket recorder as he walked around the twisted vehicle.

Suddenly, he stopped and took a measuring tape from his jacket pocket. Pulling the end of the tape, he measured twenty-nine inches from the ground to the top of the crumpled roof. As he recited the measurement into his recorder, he heard a banging sound from within the mass of metal.

"Holy…" He jumped back, shaken. The last thing he expected was any sign of life in this mess. He moved closer. A loud boom came from inside the crushed vehicle and something inside began to push the metal upward like a tent. Paul felt the blood rush from his face as he turned and ran for his car.

While he turned the key to start his sedan, a series of booms began resonating across the impound lot. His mouth gaping, he watched as the destroyed limo bounced up from the ground and land several feet closer to his car. At last, the engine started and he floored the gas pedal, spraying gravel behind him as he got as far away as he could from whatever was happening behind him.

He was just out of sight when a fist punched through the top of the limo. Then, another hand emerged. Seraphine began to tear the twisted metal away to create a larger hole. A moment later, she stepped down from the mess and onto to the gravel surface of the lot.

Emerging naked from the wreckage and into the golden light of the setting sun, she looked left to right. She raised her fists to the sky and opened her mouth, screaming, "It doesn't end here, Jacob Rune. You and your kind will pay for this with your rotting flesh! This world *will* be ours."

Continued in Rune Season II - Episode V: Sacrifice